Jerry Halv— ——— —— ———— ——————— where horses worked the fields, was nearly killed by a runaway team at age ten. At thirteen he purchased Topsy, a yellow-colored palomino mare for eighty-five hard-earned dollars. Paint, Jerry's first Appaloosa, mated with an Arabian mare, Little Connie, and initiated four full decades of speckled memories. DAKOTA MEMORY reflects Jerry's life long experience with horses and his understanding of the human condition.

Jerry is a professor in The Department of Communicative Disorders at the University of Wisconsin-River Falls. Father of five children, Jerry lives within a stone's throw of the Trimbelle, a pristine trout stream. Created in this atmosphere of tranquility, the writing of DAKOTA MEMORY ends as a bouncing spring colt trails his mother through the rapids.

Copyright 1998 by Jerry Halvorson

*All rights reserved by Jerry Halvorson and
Halvorson Farms of Wisconsin Incorporated
at Hager City, Wisconsin*

*All photographs provided by Jerry Halvorson
and David Halvorson*

ISBN 0-9664894-0-3

*Published by Halvorson Farms of Wisconsin, Inc.
Hager City, Wisconsin*

*Printed in the United States of America by
HIAWATHA DESIGN, INC.
Lake City, Minnesota*

*First Printing June, 1998
Second Printing August, 1998*

DEDICATION

To Paint, my first Appaloosa horse, who was responsible for getting this all started.

Appaloosa horses previously owned by Jerry

DAKOTA MEMORY

Jerry Halvorson

Halvorson Farms of Wisconsin, Inc.
Hager City, Wisconsin

DAKOTA COLT

Steely dust stirred around his feet and rose like smoke from a fire up his nose. Jack cautiously poked his left boot into the flat leather stirrup. With the strength of his left leg Jack hoisted his 200-pound athletic body and swinging his right leg over the Hereford saddle, the bones of his damaged knee crunched into place. Wincing with pain, Jack moved the young Appaloosa into a trot with a squeeze of his legs. North Dakota dirt covered the vertical stripes of the filly's feet and after breaking into a lope, rising dust coated the snake-skin markings on all four legs.

The circling horse wound Jack's brain tighter and tighter. The horse's rhythmic galloping jarred loose thoughts that lived in darkness next to lust. In the shadows of unconsciousness dwelled the survival instincts that Jack lived by. Like a fallen high wire acrobat with clasped hands, Jack desperately clung to the thin wire of self-preservation.

Riddles of life, love and occupation often depended upon the together motion of horse and rider for their solution. Internal struggles that were a puzzle on the ground would become readily clear on horseback. The outside of the horse was good for the inside of Jack.

While mentally preoccupied, Jack also needed to outwit an animal that multiplied his size and strength by five times. Standing harder in the stirrup, leaning backward or making a chirping noise were simple actions that Jack used in training. Raising his sleeve to brow wipe the day's sweat, the spooky young filly jolted one more shot of adrenaline into Jack's bloodstream as she shied sideways.

When he dismounted, Jack Steele's right boot puffed evening dust that hung chestnut red as yellow August sun filtered through dried particles of gumbo clay. His worn sideways cowhide boots, resurfaced with one more protective coating of North Dakota dirt, were due for another resoling. Jack released the mental pressure on the young Appaloosa by stroking in circular motions around her forehead cowlick. Most Illusion offspring displayed the swirl two inches above eye level and in the very center of the face. The filly dropped her muzzle lower and lower as Jack continued the hypnotic massage.

Cooperation was absolutely essential and trust was a must. Jack's knowledge, time and patience would convert a horse's natural actions into useful ranch performance. Separateness would yield to togetherness as the man and the horse moved in unison. The filly would appear to perform for her own enjoyment and with the slightest touch of a rein. It would almost appear that she anticipated Jack's commands through mental telepathy. True unity was the goal of completed horse training.

Jack's childhood memory still felt his father's rising and falling chest as he listened to a steadily beating heart. His sensitive child ear, pressed against the deep rumble of his dad's voice, listened to cowboy tales from the ROCKING J collection. He could still faintly hear his father describing the synchrony of Roy and Gene. Then, thinking back to his mother's bedtime tales, the images of Roy Rogers and Gene Autry intruded further. The rearing of Trigger's golden palomino body with his flowing snow-white mane, as Roy lifted his hat to salute the crowd, had been forever imprinted in Jack's long term memory. On lonely evenings, after the day's ranch work was put aside, Jack still listened to Melody Ranch records until they spun to their last groove.

Jack always saved his favorite mount for the last ride of the day. The colt's coloring looked like an Appaloosa illusion. Snowy white hair separated glossy bay spots that were larger than softballs and circled with fading halos. Vertical black stripes ran up the colt's four shins.

The equine teen-ager was circling more slowly as the edge wore off and legs wobbled with fatigue. That's the way it always worked. Only a few minutes were really valuable for training young horses. As the colt's heart girth grew, the number of loped circles would increase. Jack estimated such data with uncounted accuracy. Age would extend the colt's productive work time, but for this training session the time clock had been punched, the whistle had been blown and the pin had been pulled. The training session was over.

While dismounting, the grating of Jack's left knee bones startled the green-broke colt. Jack fell safely from the wide stirrup and rolled into a protective ball. Except for his knee, Jack's bruised body would heal, but many punishment pebbles pressed against the yielding circuits of his heart and mind.

Implanted throughout Jack's psyche were filters that screened and discarded gravel memories into his sleeping mind. His Dakota memory only wanted to recall to conscious thinking those special secrets stored in darkened cellars where sweet fruits of summer wait to nourish body and soul through dormant winters of discontent. Painful rocks occasionally stuck to the tender quarters and would be cast with their sharpness onto the wayside leaving only the passage of time and frantic activity to erode those edges that poked into his waking thought like a pointy rock to the tender arch.

Jack's thoughts flipped back to reality. Before darkness covered the ROCKING J, he had time for one more ride. With the saddle cinched there were more circles to gallop that would wind his mind even tighter. When the young colt extended into a lope, Jack again relished true unity of horse and rider. For a few precious moments there was complete coordination between two. Jack now realized that only those brief interludes made tolerable the days and weeks and months and years of mundane and masochistic survival.

Jack's loneliness helped him sweep the dirt of meaningless existence into the corners of his mind. He needed to focus on the tiny specks of positive Dakota memory that included the names of his deceased parents and the horse, Illusion. Another person, who was his first morning thought and his last evening recollection, also occupied the deepest part of Jack's nocturnal Dakota memory. Jack had loved her and imagined that she would someday return to the ROCKING J.

Evening settled. The ranch house at the ROCKING J was completely dark. Jack stood next to the shoulder of the colt he called Taconite, wishing that someone would flip the light switches. Searching in the dark for the light switch, Jack had no fear of the boogie man. He only feared what the darkness meant—lonely isolation. Maybe a remote control could be designed that would activate at least one bulb. That would make his house seem like a lived-in home.

Jack's eyes had adapted to the invading darkness. The full Moon provided light for the harvesting combines that whined in the North Dakota wheat fields. By midnight Jack's wheat field would be stubble and straw. An idling diesel engine waited to haul the grain to the Harvey, North Dakota elevator.

The colt Jack Steele was riding, a young Appaloosa with at least a hundred chestnut spots covering him from nose to toes, would be ridden through the harvested fields the next time he was saddled. Jack had cut his teeth riding Appaloosas and the ROCKING J band of Appaloosa horses had been the source of high-color for nearly a half-century.

Under his mother's tutelage, Jack had learned the entire history of the Appaloosa breed including the discovery of spotted horse carvings depicted in prehistoric cave drawings. Spanish explorers had accidentally allowed some spotted escapees to roam freely and reproduce in what would become the Western half of the United States of America. Native American people captured and trained the horses with spotted hides, but it was the Nez Perce' tribe that most valued and promoted the Appaloosa.

The Nez Perce' spoke the Sahaptian language and lived in the Snake River Valley of Idaho. By castrating inferior stallions, they had selectively bred their band of horses for desirable traits. Strength and stamina were required to climb mountains and speed was essential for hunting. At their encampments along the Palouse River, the horses became labeled "A Palouse" horse by the early French explorers and through assimilation, the two words became one. Nez Perce' horses displayed varying patterns of color. Some had snow-capped hips with no spots, others were spotted from head to toe and still others were dark-colored with white flecks.

The flashy Appaloosas, who lived in docility on the village edges, caught the eye of the early explorers. On the Louisiana Purchase Expedition, Lewis and Clarke became friends with the Nez Perce' and in their written journals, expressed surprise at the selective breeding of the Palouse horse.

Jack imagined that his father's herd stallion, Illusion, owed his black and white hide to an ancestor ridden in battle by the aging Chief Joseph. In surrender to the United States Army, the Chief spoke to his people while mounted for one last time on Illusion's leopard great-great-great grandsire. "Hear me my Chiefs. My heart is sick and sad. From where the sun now stands, I will fight no more, forever."

Carrying women and children, the sturdy Appaloosas had been capable of outrunning the United States Cavalry on a late 1800's death march. The soldiers, who only cared for themselves, finally captured the Nez Perce' only 40 miles from Canada. The year was 1877.

The horses were disbanded and not being selectively bred, nearly vanished as the distinctive breed they had been during the Eighteenth and Nineteenth Centuries. During the 1930's, a man by the name of Claude Thompson who hailed from Oregon tried to resurrect the Appaloosa horse. One of his first horses was named Red Eagle, a cross between an Appaloosa mare and an Arabian stallion.

In the next thirty years, other breeders would jump on the bandwagon by infusing Appaloosa color into horses of other saddle horse breeds. In 1938, a registry called The Appaloosa Horse Club of America formalized the keeping of pedigrees and by the 1950's, the endangered coat patterns, varying from a few white hip specks to full leopard color, again speckled the country. Jack looked at the evening sky and imagined smiling tears on the cheeks of Chief Joseph as he rode through the Happy Hunting Grounds on his black leopard stallion. The horse was Illusion.

Sparse mane fibers stuck from the colt's neck. Most of the genuine Appaloosas grew only short manes and tails. Some sported tails so hairless that they became labeled "rat tails." Bony tails banged their hips hairless in fly time. Those original Nez Perce' characteristics would eventually be bred out as signs of inferiority. But Jack loved them.

Running his hand over the colt's rump and down the leg, Jack examined a rope burned pastern. The colt's ankle would soon be 100% and he had learned a lesson on the way to the abrasion that would someday save his life. He had learned to accept restraint. With the bloodline of his pliable grandsire coursing under his spotted hide and the teaching of a third generation Steele molding his habits, the acquisition had been rapid and the retention permanent.

Jack had trained at least a hundred colts that celebrated Illusion as their sire or grandsire. Their dispositions, moldable as hot plastic, were complimented by mottled skins and vividly contrasting coat patterns. Every one had a natural lead change even at a slow lope and their necks were naturally arched for proper collection.

Jack stepped back to examine the colt's conformation and as he thought, squeezed the pain from his knee. He knew two things for sure. His knee was shot for good and there would never be another horse like Illusion. Uncle John knew that too. He wondered if anyone would ever be able to understand the real story of the famous stallion. Jack knew only one person that could really understand but she was not in his recent life and didn't know about his knee injury either. Her name was Danni. Danni Penfield.

She also loved horses. Hot-blooded horses like Arabians and Thoroughbreds. Despite the years of separation, she kept a secret place in his mind. Jack guessed that no one else needed to know about his thoughts and he disguised the swirls of his inner-self.

Eventually, the Appaloosa population dwindled like autumn leaves before the southward sun. They fell lifeless as killer pens swelled with high priced horsemeat. Danni left one winter day to tend to her sick father and although he had tried to stay in contact with her, it seemed that she had disappeared into a time chasm like the spotted horses. After all these years Jack still rode Illusion-bred Appys, but Danni seemed gone forever.

Jack's mind scanned pages of horse experiences and stopped in a chapter that featured his first Appaloosa, Paint. A truckload of horses shipped from the Cheyenne Indian Reservation in Wyoming arrived at the local sales barn in Harvey, North Dakota. He imagined Paint, a yearling colt being shipped in a double-bottomed semi with the older and larger horses, getting squashed until his breathing muscles could barely function. By taking half breaths, Paint had averted certain suffocation. That's probably why he was so tough. Paint had survived like a slave on a rolling ship with little air, lots of guts and hope.

Stepping off the young colt, Jack's hand searched without thinking for the latigo and bracing his legs toward the saddle, Jack lifted the flexible leather strap through a punched hole and pulled the loose end around two turns. Every good training session would have as its reward the loosening of the cinch immediately after the ride. His trainer comrades thought a horse could be rewarded for a lead change or a sudden stop made shortly before the released cinch pressure. But Jack knew better. The pressure release was late by large seconds and would only reward dismounting.

Jack empathized with his horses. He had known pleasure and pain and in his personal relationships had been stung more than soothed. He wished for the pleasure of the blizzard and wondered why the calm after the storm had to end so soon. Like a migrating spirit, his soul mate vanished in a snow cloud. When Danni disappeared behind the roaring engine of the diesel snowplow, Jack thought for sure that he would see her again. Now, Danni seemed everlastingly beyond his reach.

Jack realized that there was no way to really understand another person or to be understood. "Know yourself," the ancient Greek motto, described the essence of Jack's existence. He wished for an equal understanding of Danni. He had once believed that Danni Penfield and Jack Steele were forever bound in a unity of thought. Now, he wasn't sure.

Since Danni left, Jack was never really at peace with his thinking, but like rolling stones on a streambed, the rough edges of his pain had dulled. During the daylight hours he could distract himself with his active existence. At the end of a hard day's work, however, the dropping sun and rising moon reminded him of a Big Dipper memory that searched nightly for expression in Jack's dreams. The aching of his heart only yielded to nocturnal fantasy.

Jack's Philosophy major helped him understand some enigmas, but others remained a mystery. He now recognized that horse training had become a weird combination of mysticism and behaviorism—magic and science. Jack was still puzzled by his own discontent. Why, after all these years, couldn't Jack Steele be as happy as his horses and simply eliminate all negative thoughts?

Self-survival was a horse's friend and Jack's enemy. With the mental risks that Jack pursued, both his heart and body were vulnerable. His survival attempts had become self-destructive. If only his mind could learn what his heart already knew. Jack was not the least embarrassed as he talked to the colt beside him. "Taconite, you don't realize how lucky you are to be stupid. Can I trade places with you?"

Fatigue was gnawing at Jack's flesh and when his body was weak, his mind was strong. Soon it would be dark and all his thoughts would turn inward as they did every time the sun dropped. That's when he thought about Danni the most.

The reddening sun had turned against the west edge of the Earth. Dust that stirred around the colt's hoofs was imperceptible as their unitary silhouettes ambled slowly toward the barn. Moon shadows extended to their maximum length as light dew settled and darkening stillness invaded the ROCKING J.

Jack blew dust away from his nose that churned from the colt's hoofs. Jack remembered that his father always said "hoofs," instead of the more proper "hooves." Only novices in the horse world said the "V". There were lots of horse words like that. Jim Steele, one of the "make it the hard way" ranchers also said "colt" to mean both sexes of a young horse.

Flickering in his memory was another horse experience in which he learned the meaning of the term "pipe smoker," in horse lingo. Jack and his dad were looking to buy a mate for Charlie, a big sorrel Belgian gelding. At a local sales barn, a particularly zealous horse trader was trying to convince Jim Steele that a large workhorse was the horse to buy. Even though he was a perfect match in color, size and conformation, Jack's father never nodded his head when the bidding started. After the sale, Jack's logical question needed an analytical answer. "Dad, why didn't you buy that big sorrel gelding? He'd a been a perfect match for Charlie and we could have sleigh rides again."

Jim Steele chuckled as he explained to his curious son, "That horse jockey was trying to sell the horse 'cause he was a runaway. Did you see how both corners of his mouth had big grooves? He got those from pulling on the bit. That's what you call a "pipe smoker" 'cause it looks like an old man who's had a pipe hanging from the corner of his mouth for too long."

Jack's thinking never seemed to stop. How could dirt separate into such small particles? After the work was done there would be time to ponder. But for right now, the training horses had to be fed and watered. Even after the riding part of training was finished, there was more training. The horse's brain, like his own, was always happening.

Horses learn from their experiences, even in the isolation of a box or tie stall. Cooped up, like a prisoner in confinement, the horse would learn to be patient and to depend upon his guarding master. Native instincts would be suppressed in favor of domestication. In the isolation of his stall the horse would soon magnify every detail of incarceration and quickly become as institutionalized as a prisoner with a life sentence. Jack always used his thoughts as a refuge. Maybe horses did the same—especially the good ones.

By close observation, Jack had learned to tell which horses would be more pliable even before their formal training began. But good genetics was even more important than Jack's judgment. His father had always said, "The apple don't fall far from the tree." Then the wiser Steele would always say, "If you want to know how a young horse is going to mature, just check out the pedigree."

Jack wrapped a twine string around the colt's neck and pressed a forefinger on the colt's chest. Backing into his stall was a last, formal acknowledgment of being willing to learn. Then, as Jack placed his hand on the colt's nose, he noticed an improvement. For the first time, the young Appaloosa's neck flexed when pressure was placed on his nose. By doing what horsemen call "flexing at the poll," the colt was demonstrating compliance. "Cooperation," Jack thought out loud, "is the greatest thing in the world, but so seldom attained."

Jack always made mental notes of such things, keeping them catalogued for future use. Some time every smidgen of knowledge would be important. Maybe knowing a small fact would simply speed up training or at the farthest end of the continuum, save his life from a dangerous colt. The one he'd been riding was like molding soft clay, but tomorrow he would need all the knowledge and skill he could muster to educate an outlaw he was training for a neighbor.

Clay remains pliable and iron is almost never. Even though the principles of training remained constant, the material changed. The day would come when he would have only a moment to bend the iron mind of some unknown outlaw. Maybe tomorrow the Steele that was in his name could transform from raw iron ore the habits of the horse he called Taconite.

Jack's boots stepped on gravel. He looked down the quarter mile driveway to the county road that would soon be covered with evening dusk. His logical thinking disappeared like the vanishing point on an artist's canvas. In the night's stillness, brain thoughts about horses from today, yesterday and forever anonymously gathered to await Jack's evening dreams. It was too dark to see the county road.

The hour was right for thoughts to stream freely from his limbic lobe; that emotional, animalistic part of the human thought process that thinks in tangled and fragmented sentences and speaks half-said words absent of beginnings and endings.

Just there because the colors exist when black and white won't do and when he was sick as a child he saw yellow sunflowers that still came to his eyes when he was feverish or when he got his bell rung in football when most people said they saw stars but he saw sunflowers that came one upon the other getting larger and larger until they went completely into his being and there were long streams of round yellow lights with holes in the middle that would last until his fever or the head injury went away.

Turning his eyes toward his mind and removing himself from the outside world, the horse's muscles moved under the loose skin jerking away big black horse flies that were as big as bees and when he sat on that untanned hide first as he sat bareback as a child and then with a new saddle from Christmas and pulling at the work horse's tail before he knew how to say "horsey" and watching the thirsty horses' ears snap back and forth while his sharp child eyes watched them drink water and throwing the harnesses on their backs before he knew the names of the harness parts and seeing the black mare sprawled on the ground with the broken leg and hearing his mother cry because she was such a good horse and seeing his father's disgust at the drunk driver that hit her and watching the black mare walk pigeon toed as she pulled the load of hay and seeing the rendering truck pick her up.

Primal feelings had crowded Jack's intellect into the background of his brain waves. His untamed emotions that reasoned wildly or not at all, sought constantly for free expression. Like a wild range stallion in sudden confinement, his unrestrained spirit fought against the inhibitions of his intellect.

The high-pitched whinny of a newborn colt snapped Jack's mind back into reality.

Jack walked toward the house. He knew what would be for supper.

A black and white spotted Appaloosa hide greeted his entrance to the ranch house. It had hung on the same wall for more than a decade and Jack hardly noticed its presence even though most visitors wondered about its questionable artistic taste. Only Jack and Uncle John knew the complete story behind the tanned hide and they weren't sharing. There was one partial exception—Danni. Now he wasn't sure if he should have confided his most private thoughts with her either. It was some consolation to his guilty conscience that even Danni hadn't been told the entire story about the most famous horse of the Dakotas.

Danni only knew Illusion's history as a breeding stallion and how he had saved the ROCKING J from bankruptcy as a sire of leopard-skinned Appaloosas. She knew that his progeny had been advertised in *Appaloosa News*, a national magazine for Appy lovers, and that Jack's mother did most of the marketing of the weanlings through correspondence. But Jack was careful. He and Uncle John had taken an oath that they had both honored. No one outside the family would ever know the whole story about the death of Illusion. His memory was preserved adequately enough on the porch wall at the ranch house entrance.

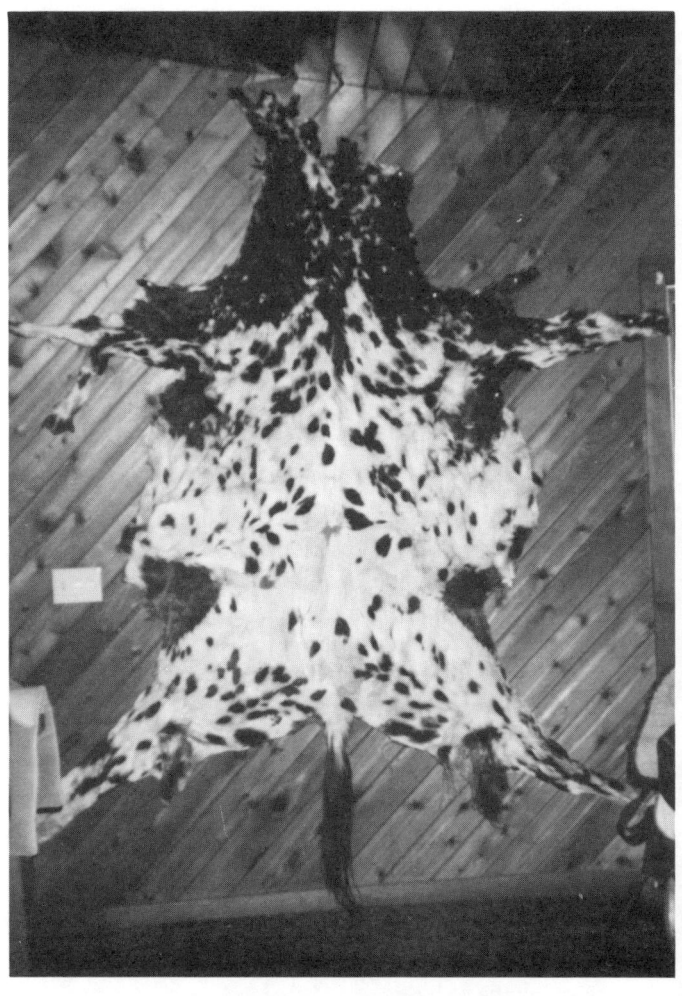

ILLUSION, herd stallion of the ROCKING J, hanging in his preserved state on the porch wall

The toils of training had created a hollow feeling in Jack's stomach and the puppy that was tangled in his ankles was always hungry. Past the weaning slump, Young Pal wolfed up any morsels that weren't for human consumption. Not that food was the only need Jack sensed, but a good meal would salve the soul. The young Australian Shepherd would sleep on a full stomach with twitching feet and whining vocal cords as he herded the phantoms of his nightmares. His John The Baptist forerunner, Old Pal, had sacrificed his 14 year-old skull to a striking front foot. Slow reflexes made fast departures on the ROCKING J.

Before going out to do evening chores, a pot of potatoes and carrots mixed with some venison chunks had been stirred together and placed on the back lids of the old wood cookstove. Sizzling droplets of water spilled over the kettle's edge, creating a steam of nostril energy. The smell started to restore his strength. The slow boiling smell of celery reminded him of the seasonings that he had submerged in the cold water two hours before sunset. The potatoes weren't peeled.

The phone rang before he could even remove his boots. The night air at 40 degrees was extra cool for August and made the soup booya smell like it should be devoured rather than eaten. Trying to remove his boots before the ringing stopped, Jack jerked the left one too rapidly and heard the grinding of bones that cartilage no longer protected. After ten hours of ranch work, his boots, socks and feet were laminated together with grit and sweat. He grabbed the receiver by the fifth ring.

He knew who he hoped it would be. Most of the time the phone was a nuisance—an intrusion into his privacy and a demand on his time. Jack had learned to like living alone.

Wood cookstove of the ROCKING J

At least that's what his neighbors believed. That once-in-a-great-while call from someone he really cared about made him pay the phone bill. He knew better than to be a nicely trained white rat for a telephone company. But he had been brainwashed and like most other people had a disease he called "telephonitis." He couldn't resist picking up the receiver. Even if he knew better he couldn't resist. Only one other thing was like that. "Danni. Danni Penfield." Jack whispered hoarsely to himself.

It had been a long time. As he reflected, there was not enough room in his brain for things other than horses. The only people who seemed to make a difference were friends whose camaraderie had been established with the mixed scent of shavings and horses. Once there was a girl like that. The phone call couldn't be from her since he hadn't heard from her in over eight years. In fact, it was eight years, seven months and six days. Maybe that, 8-7-6, was a countdown omen and Danni was on the other end of the line.

The phone call was from a telemarketing agency advertising windows. Not exactly what he needed. Rattling off a memorized lingo, the sweet female voice sounded better than it should have. Maybe it was his need to just talk to someone. Horses were fine and all, but real human flesh was what Jack wanted in the house. Like a "sacked-out" horse that learns to accept an array of frightening experiences, Jack felt subdued by his own memories. Years of loneliness had trapped his thinking in webs of tangled memory.

He hadn't spoken to Danni in so long that the cobwebs were sagging with age. By now, she had probably taken to other things. Jack remembered her tender touch. He could picture her riding a black Arabian stallion with nothing to control the horse, but a decorative lead rope. Guided by

Danni in a bridleless routine, the lathered Arab was dripping with sweat. Distended veins, pulsing under his skin, were glistening with sweat as the Arabian's heart swelled. Jack could barely tolerate the memory of Danni.

It wasn't her voice on the phone and he wasn't sure if it would be recognizable or that he would even want to hear it again. The sound of Danni's voice might be too painful. Like everyone else, Jack looked for pleasure and tried to avoid pain.

He knew the pain-pleasure principle first hand. Without one the other is meaningless. Jack had known both the thrill of his all too short relationship with Danni and the agony of his forced separation. His horses were hammered into shape through repetition on the anvil of experience. Jack sometimes wondered why he couldn't accept as truth what his horses learned so easily.

Jack was convinced that animals only learned at the most simple, reflexive level. Reward created learned habits and pleasant memories that imprinted deep traces in the horse's mind. Punished acts stung the brain with painful memory. Jack quickly understood such elegant, yet uncomplicated, logic. Possessing higher powers of thinking, he was worried about relinquishing simple savage instincts in favor of evolving intellect. Like every other bright person, Jack knew that he had the mental ability to reason away such simple truths.

Horses were different. Having been domesticated for their athletic ability, they lost pitifully to the meager intelligence of childlike people, chimpanzees and puppies. With Young Pal panting at his master's feet, Jack whispered. "Why then, is this puppy so much happier than I am?" Jack's internal question had puzzled even the greatest thinkers.

Jack tilted his lithe, muscular upper body to the right, relieving the radiating ache from his left knee. Recalling a quote from an existentialist philosopher, his hand reached for the aspirin bottle. Jack whispered to himself. "Logic is doubtless, unshakable, but it cannot withstand a man who wants to go on living." That was Jack's prescription for this moment.

House windows were being promoted by the sweet voice on the phone. Maybe he'd ask if she sold internal windows that let you look into your own soul and the hearts of others. Jack refrained and simply explained that he didn't need any windows right now.

That was not the fantasy phone call he wanted. Yet, Jack's mind had twisted the mildly aversive phone ring and the pleasant female voice into a pleasurable experience, triggering distant memories of Danni and creating a hope for tomorrow. During his sleeping hours, a different reality would intrude, but for now, Jack's nostalgic thoughts had pleasantly subdued the aspirin-resistant pain of his lonely and aching heart.

The cookstove fire was nearly down to embers. Jack indulged. The simmering venison stew filled his stomach and replenished strength to his angular six-foot one frame. No one would guess his age to be only 29. Tonight's nourishment could not undo yesterday's suns.

Hours in the sun had forever tanned his face. Jack's dark wavy hair had grown longer since college. In the summers, a shock of sun-bleached curls hung loosely over the front of his forehead matching the changing color of his thick eyebrows. Even the harsh North Dakota winters were too short for his skin to become winter white. His walk was still quick, but tilted to the right.

After graduating from High School, Jack had enrolled at Nebraska where he had a free ride on a football scholarship. Four years and two knee surgeries later, academics became more important than football. Even though his knee was barely good enough to do summer rodeo, Jack's mind was sharper than ever. His major in Philosophy seemed to the other cowboys inconsistent with steer wrestling and calf roping. They razzed Jack, giving him the nickname "Xenophon."

The rough and tumble cowboys thought Jack's gentle ways of taming and restraining young horses resembled the famous horseman and philosopher of ancient Greece. Jack explained to his cowpoke friends how Xenophon trained his charges for battle. Xenophon's principles of horse training, that had eluded nearly all third millenium horse trainers, were branded on Jack's experience ledger. Jack fully realized that, as long ago as three hundred fifty-five years before the birth of Christ, there was another deep thinker who understood horses.

The sizzling water on the stovetop had been converted into humidity and there was absolute silence in the ROCKING J ranch house. Young Pal was wrapped in a sleeping ball on Jack's lap. The twitching pup, so contentedly chasing dream cattle, helped shrink Jack's loneliness. The isolation that pleased him temporarily would later bore Jack and devour his thinking like a cancer to the brain. After-work fatigue was good for contemplation and short naps. Reclined in his easy chair, Jack was able to figure out a problem that had been unsolvable outside. Similarly, Jack could see some human dilemmas more clearly from horseback.

Jack rubbed a new sore spot on his left knee. Earlier that day, a barn sour colt had fallen while circling to the left. Jack's leg had been pinned under the colt's dropped shoulder. Flattening the top of a galloped circle, the colt had simply tried to return home. Instinct impelled the colt to seek herd protection.

Jack projected his feelings to the young, insecure colt and understood the colt's need for companionship. Jack only resorted to the simple comforts of his bachelor house to fulfill basic human needs and stimulate his thinking. He had lots of friends, but none close enough to listen and lend comfort in time of lonely desperation. Only Danni would understand. Like himself, the colt was simply running for the security and protection of his comrades. Jack wished he could run to Danni.

Rather than struggling to free himself, Jack had simply waited for the colt to get to his feet. The only lasting casualty was the stirrup on Jack's Hereford saddle that was sprung crooked. The abrasion on Jack's knee would heal. Elevating and icing would reduce pain and shrink the swelling, but tomorrow would be another day and a knee without cartilage never really recovers.

Jack knew better than to assume that horses could be treated as pets. Undomesticated nature and superior athletic ability made even the tamest horse potentially dangerous. With his newest knee injury, it would be best to have an extra hand tomorrow. He'd try to recruit someone who was not only capable, but also totally unafraid. Stretch lived just down the road in an old trailer house.

According to the clock, it was time to watch Monday night football. For the first time since supper, Jack clicked the remote control. With his left leg propped up on the footrest of his recliner and an ice bag dripping to the floor below his knee, Jack reminisced. All the neighbors said Jack would make the NFL and play on Sunday instead of Saturday. That aspiration ended the day he caught a pass and was sandwiched. One tackled high—the other low. His left knee was in the middle. His future-minded daydream of traveling from North Dakota to Nebraska to Wisconsin was now only a vicarious Monday night fantasy. Sensing the residual pain in his knee, it seemed a hallucination. The Green Bay Packers didn't need him tonight—or ever.

Jack watched wide receivers on TV and his memory shortened to a flash as his fantasy gave way to reality. His left knee that was bone against bone would still tolerate ranch work if his aspirin bottle didn't run dry. There was always the faint hope of some miracle cartilage surgery. But by then, he'd be too old.

Of necessity, Jack had reactivated his parents' ranch. Uncle John, now in the local nursing home, had ridden too many broncs and painted his leathery-tanned face with too many sunsets. Barely surviving on the sales of the weaned calves in the fall, Jack trained other people's horses for pay and his own to sell.

Jack's cow-puncher reputation was uncertain, but his fame as a horse trainer was becoming a local legend. He had trained horses for people as far away as Chicago, Illinois— close to where Danni lived.

The old time ranchers didn't quite understand the way Jack worked with his horses. Instead of bucking out the colts and risking injury to both the horse and rider, Jack's early training emphasized desensitization. Jack called this training "avoidance prevention." Jack's training horses were not allowed to successfully avoid any frightening stimulus, whether learned or instinctive. Every horse Jack educated—even the old pet horses he accepted for retraining—learned like the Pentecostal gospel song said, "To trust and obey for there's no other way to be happy in Jesus." The horses didn't know about Jesus so they learned about Jack.

Frank Gifford's voice would suspend Jack's horse thinking, but it only intensified the image of Danni. She had met Jack in college. He was a wide receiver from a North Dakota ranch and she was an intellectual from suburban Chicago.

Jack laughed out loud. His aloneness could not stop this enjoyment. Remembering Danni's reaction to Curly, his grandpa's life-like preserved horse, Jack walked into the living room to see a white horse hide, with head attached, lying lengthwise on the brown carpet. Baskir Curlys were a rare breed and when Grandpa's favorite horse died, Curly became an almost living, living room rug. When Danni had first seen Curly's fake glass eyes and real-looking pointy ears, she almost resigned her job as temporary housekeeper. Jack's laugh subsided as another Dakota memory slipped into the retrievable file.

They happened to meet in a Sociology class. Fate could never have been more kind. Jack's posture of sticking his cowboy boots into the middle of the aisle of the large auditorium caused Danni a near fall as she said, "Hey cowboy, your boots are obstructing my path."

Having noticed her before, Jack was quick to reply with a prepared invitation that sounded spontaneous. "You wouldn't have to climb over me if you'd take the chair right here."

She sat down next to him. Jack didn't trust women and had never allowed himself to get too close emotionally. With Danni seated beside him there was a smashing in Jack's mind that shocked him into childish regression. Maybe it was the smell of the shavings that stuck with Danni after she bedded her horse. Coupled with the slight scent of Danni's perfume, Jack remembered that his pony died and his mother cried.

Jack nostalgically rehearsed the short story by John Steinbeck, "The Red Pony," in which a young boy's pony died of strangles. Not wanting Danni to read his thoughts, Jack turned his head pretending to be interested in the lecture. The images stood vividly in his mind and would surely be visible on his face.

Louder than the professor's lecture, the child in Jack's listening soul could still hear the engine of the rendering truck as it backed into the yard and the grunting of the greasy man who hooked the cable around his dead pony's neck. Gently but firmly, his mother's hand restrained Jack from rushing to Wildfire's decaying body. Like Steinbeck's hero, he wanted to kill the buzzard that was consuming his love.

Breaking from his mother's grasp, his fleet child legs chased the truckload of dead animals until the flat Dakota horizon diminished his Wildfire to a pencil point. Then there was nothing, but his empty lungs to scream "Wildfire" years before Michael Murphy sang the pop song with the pained words, "he ran calling Wildfire." First losses are most painful. Eventually, every heart will harden.

Danni sat quietly beside him. A strange sense of primal security came from this woman, sitting only inches from him. She seemed like the promise his mother had never kept. Yet, his mind wound tighter and seemed unable to relax. Jack never received the replacement pony his mother guaranteed. He remembered not being able to stop crying. In Steinbeck's writing, a living full-term colt had been ripped from its dying mother's womb with a slashing knife. Jack thought, "What a way to replace his dead red pony." There was no living substitute for Jack's pony. There was only the stabbing hurtful memory of lost love.

This time the blade to Jack's heart was gentle and kind. Danni would not hurt him. Unwilling to reveal his true inner-self, Jack substituted a neutralizing remark for his real thoughts. "The way you smell of horses, you sure would have liked the pony I had in North Dakota."

Jack's outward expression of confidence was like double-layered veneer that protected a vulnerable interior. His hard red oak shell looked impenetrable, but underneath was a soft sensitive psyche made of weeping willow. There were so many thoughts that never became speech and so many feelings that never became action. Jack's inner sensitivity had increased his capacity to sense the earliest manifestations and the slightest indications of other peoples' emotion.

With premature haste he roughed out some conclusions about Danni. He would not have to thrash the buzzards who tore the flesh of his red pony or cry hysterically when the pregnant mare was struck four inches above eye center or see the meat grinder make mink food of his pony or feel rejected when Wildfire wasn't replaced. Danni's immediate presence soothed the surfacing pain.

He wondered about her history of horses and men. Would she like his ranch? He could already imagine her athletic frame accompanying him at chore time. On days when rain stopped the plow, they could fire-up the cookstove and as Danni cooked with nothing but her apron on, share the contentment of the ROCKING J ranch house. Jack glanced quickly at her face to see any reaction. Romantic thoughts swelled and then consumed his visage. Danni brushed away long black hair, revealing the deepness of her dark brown eyes and as she turned, the swishing sound of her ponytail forced Jack to stare all the way through Danni's eyes into the deepest parts of her brain.

At that moment Danni knew. And so did Jack. For both, it was love at first glance.

They left class together. Breakfast awaited them in the school cafeteria and as they waited in line and as they loaded their trays and as they ate, their conversation deepened. Jack had never talked to a woman that made him feel so comfortable. He thought back to his first childish horse training. Jack had instinctively learned to observe subtle signs of companionship. Wildfire, his little red pony, would turn toward him as he submitted to being caught. Then he would start moving his mouth and making licking noises as he nuzzled the small boy's pockets looking for sugar lumps stolen from the kitchen. While cradling the pony's head over his shoulder and rubbing his forehead, Jack listened for the long sigh of contentment that meant his pony loved him.

Maybe he could learn to really trust again. The day Wildfire succumbed to colic, Jack said good-bye to something deep inside himself. He wasn't quite sure if it was childhood or unconditional love. Danni invited him to reach out and touch the private memory of Wildfire. Buried in a private section of his brain reserved only for himself and Wildfire, Jack had discovered another person. Danni. Danni Penfield.

Philosophy class was Jack's favorite. It caused him to think about everything, but lately everything was related to Danni. Since the death of his parents, and within the realm of all human experience, two beacons guided Jack's ship safely to shore. In an essay for his Philosophy class, Jack described how his life had been permanently altered at age 17. It was at that time he realized that self-survival is not enough. Before his parents were killed, he had proclaimed with juvenile certainty that self-preservation is the only real and essential component to happiness.

One drunk driver convinced him that contentment is never complete in isolation. His essay described with frightening clarity the grief and loneliness that loss brings. It was not until then that Jack realized ultimate happiness included both his own physical, emotional and mental health, as well as, the relationships with those social beings that he loved. Danni was first on Jack's list.

One day after Sociology 101 Jack handed Danni a hand written note. It said in childlike poetic rhyme:

"When sunset dies on western land
I know that on some foreign sand
The tiring day has just begun
And my days work is almost done." jack

The verse had been written in Jack's sophomore high school English class. The assignment had been to write a short verse that explained the meaning of existence. Jack's fellow students thought long and hard, coming up with a few meaningless personal quotes.

The tenth grade teacher had read Jack's poem to the entire class and asked Jack to explain its content. Fearlessly, Jack explained to his classmates that working the land and the cattle made the horses necessary. When the sun went down, even though his work was done, there was more to do. The solitude of Dakota nights spun the globe in Jack's reflective mind. Even when his day's work was done, someplace it had just begun.

Jack wondered if an upper-middle class daughter of a neurosurgeon from suburban Chicago could understand the thinking of a North Dakota rancher. He knew she cared, but could she understand the drudgery of ranch work.

By November, Jack's work ethic had already paid off. The coaching staff at Nebraska had decided to pull his red shirt status. Because of injuries to other wide receivers, Jack had been activated, pronto. Jack's long galloping stride and his home state gained him the nickname: "Dakota Colt." Sometimes, the guys just called him "Colt" and sometimes, the coaches called him just "Dakota," but the newspapers always called him "The Dakota Colt." His sticky fingers made the quarterback's job easy. Any ball in his vicinity belonged to Nebraska. His hard hitting and fearless approach to football, acquired working on the Dakota tundra, seemed to make him impervious to pain and injury. Lighting up the sports page with circus catches, Jack's reflexes befuddled his defenders.

As a college freshman, Jack played like a pro and Danni was his greatest fan. She never missed a game, except for one time. Before Thanksgiving, Dr. George Penfield, Danni's father, had become a patient himself. His heart was failing and he was hospitalized. Only her sick father could intercept Jack's passes.

Danni returned to campus after Thanksgiving. There was a gnawing inside her stomach as she stepped off the plane.

Jack was at football practice and she would have to wait to see him until evening. Except for a few new linebacker-caused contusions, Jack had not changed, but he could tell at first glance that something was really different about Danni. Without saying even the first word, Jack wrapped both arms around Danni's shoulders and she buried her sobbing face in his chest. Holding her silently seemed to quell the internal storm. No one but Jack—and maybe not even Jack—would be able to understand.

Jack's listening helped. First there were only a few words. Having experienced the grief of losing both parents, Jack knew first hand the anguish Danni would feel if her father died.

Danni's halting utterances jerked as she tried minute upon minute to suppress her crying. Jack squeezed the bear hug tighter and sucked Danni's pain into his own being.

Instantly shooting his senses into a revolving scurry Jack's mind kicked away it's barriers and he could still visualize his mother's sharp eyes now closed with her hair so neatly arranged for just one more time and his father's leathery face made plastic with make-up with his huge hands minus one finger folded too neatly on his sleepless chest and the cars with all their lights lit carrying ranch neighbors that had hanger marks in their suit coats and the bugler that played before the twenty-one gun salute and all the hugging in the church basement with the ladies serving sandwiches and Jell-O and potato salad and one large hot dish and a silver tray full of homemade pieces of cake and his friends dressed up for the first time with nothing to say because they didn't know how and then everyone was gone and only the empty loneliness and grief and Uncle John stayed.

Of course he could understand. Every day he wished he could return to the ROCKING J and his parents' comfort. Only the medicine known as tincture of time would heal these wounds. The Blue Vitriol his father routinely dabbed on horses' wire cuts looked good to the people who didn't know better, but sage horse practitioners knew that doing nothing was equally effective. The inside of Jack knew the same thing. All the meaningless rituals make a pleasant outward appearance, but the natural healing process requires time.

The last games of the year drifted into Cornhusker history and Dakota Colt, the freshman, became statistics, stories and post-game highlights. Other Big Eight wide receivers had their numbers compared and were found wanting. He was no longer just a great high school football player who also liked academics and happened to be from a small Dakota ranch.

Jack's shoulders were filled with weight training muscle, the hams of his legs hung when relaxed and his brain was crammed with higher education. Jack's future spread before him as though he was resuming a pleasant dream that had been unfairly interrupted. The nightmares of past traumatic experiences were losing control of Jack's mind as Danni stood solidly beside him.

Before the last game of the year, Danni invited Jack to her grandfather's retirement ranchette. Her grandpa was gone for the weekend and she had been assigned the chore duties. To Jack, the small amount of work seemed to be nothing but play and he joked with Danni about how clean she picked the stalls and about putting blankets on the horses. Danni smiled, enjoying the special attention, wishing she could share more times like these with this man she loved.

Late Sunday evening, after chores, they burned a pile of dried brush behind the barn and as their eyes watched sparks ascending skyward, they noticed the Big Dipper. They sat as one on a common wood stump with jackets opened to the fire sensing the opposing December chill entering from behind. In the darkness just beyond the campfire a horse nickered. Danni pulled Jack closer with her open jacket exposing her breasts to the touch of Jack's chest.

The fire was no longer needed. As the night deepened, the Big Dipper started to tilt and was then covered with clouds. Sometime before midnight, a light sleeting rain bent the tree branches and the frozen electrical high-line wires crackled in the wind.

Jack and Danni would wait until morning to return to school. Only a fool would risk travel on glare ice when Grandpa's comfortable house was stocked with food and had running water. Besides, they needed to baby sit the house since it was unlikely that Danni's elderly grandparents would try to travel in such weather. Old Man Winter had decided it was time. The sleet storm sounded scary. As they curled into each other's arms, Jack told her of far away North Dakota blizzards that made the storm just outside the window seem like the Fourth of July. Jack told Danni about the ROCKING J and Uncle John. He never mentioned Illusion.

DANNI

Narrow rubber tires mounted on silver-spoked wheels rolled the chair slowly down the long corridor. Others were lined up against the wall. Each wheelchair carried an invalid between the two large wheels. Some stared impersonally with unfocused eyes, others attempted to eat with drool-coated mouths and a few squirmed with confused agitation.

Danni remembered her first visit to a head trauma unit. Her uncle had been injured in a car wreck and after the accident was diagnosed as TBI, traumatic brain injury. She was only a teen-ager at the time and was impressionable. The picture of her father's once athletic brother strapped into a wheelchair with far away eyes and drooling mouth continued daily to resurrect her professional calling.

Danni Penfield's personal vendetta to become a Doctor of Physical Medicine and Rehabilitation traced to a fall taken while jumping her Thoroughbred at the riding academy. Unable to clear the jump cleanly, the horse propelled Danni over his shoulder. She remembered the sensation of flying through the air. That had happened many times and would again. Danni was a tomboy who loved taking physical risks. The soft ground couldn't hurt her.

Probability caught up with Danni. Three feet above the ground she was still awake. Then there was nothing. In the twilight of her awakening, Danni knew she was actually feeling the vibrations of the screaming ambulance siren. Danni recognized only faintly that something was wrong. She tried to sit up, but couldn't move because straps held her tightly to a board. Her head was immobilized and hurt so much she thought her skull would burst. Her lower jaw stung with pain. The gash on the point of her chin made her whole lower jaw seem strangely anesthetized. It felt novocaine numb.

As the paramedics transferred Danni to the emergency room she heard them talking in scrambled words about the horse's knee and how it had made contact with her chin. They said that even Ali couldn't stand that kind of punch. As the strange people moved their mouths their speech made more and more sense until she knew the awakening had occurred.

The horse's knee had cold-cocked her like a huge Mike Tyson uppercut. Iron Mike weighed 215 pounds, with not even one-fifth the power of the eleven hundred-pound Thoroughbred gelding. In a few more minutes, the faces started to look familiar. The people in white were doctors and nurses, who seemed to be trying to help by asking questions that insulted her intelligence, but were still too difficult. Who is the President? What day of the week is it? What is your name?

Unlike her uncle, Danni came around in a few hours and was released directly from the emergency room. But the strange darkness, the twilight and the awakening were stamped forever. She would always be on a first name basis with head trauma. Her professional autobiography would be altered by a Thoroughbred's steel knee. Later, Danni's personal biography would be written by a man of Steele. Jack Steele.

There was another, larger factor that influenced her career choice. Danni's father, a neurosurgeon, had set an example that his daughter would try to emulate in her academic and professional life. But when it came to horses, Danni did not listen to her father or anyone else.

Dr. George Penfield warned Danni about horses. He had seen more than one patient who was not as lucky as Danni. Danni's attachment to horses was like a genetic flaw; probably a predisposition passed from one of her grandfathers who was an uncertified horse doctor, a poor man's veterinarian.

Until she went to college even men were second class citizens when compared to horses. At Nebraska there had been this one man whose camaraderie for equines had been jointly shared. Jack Steele had become more than a friend and as she walked down the line of patients, she wondered what had ever happened to the cowboy that had frozen his image in her mind during a North Dakota blizzard.

Danni's practical experience, while a resident at The Mayo Clinic in Rochester, toppled many of her preconceived notions about what it would be like to be a doctor. Her ambition of providing salvation to head trauma patients had been tempered by the time she reached her fourth year of residency.

Danni had become hardened to the woes of traumatically brain-injured people whose candleflame of life dimly flickered. The patients, oblivious to the passage of time and with infant-like dependency, lay unaware of the near-empty hourglass at their bedside. Numbered hours seemed to carelessly sift away the few remaining sand grains. Standing beside motionless beds, the patients' relatives consumed candies and demanded that the hourglass be inverted by the expertise of Dr. Danni Penfield.

As she turned the corner to get off the four-lane highway at Zumbrota, Danni recalled with amusement her idealism as a young medical student in Physical Medicine and Rehabilitation. An occasional hourglass could be turned by modern medicine, but with most TBI patients, there was only hope for a miracle.

Along the plastered hallway were cheering-up pictures and bulletin boards with easy to read notices that meant nothing to the patients whose reticular formations, lying in a frayed network throughout their brainstems, refused to provide adequate signals to control sleep and wakefulness. The young adult patients, who managed to break from the next to death silence, had mouths that drooled strings of saliva and eyes that looked with dilation as their faces drooped in sadness. Kissing, twinkling and smiling were words for that once-in-a-great-while patient who managed to recover enough to reach the exit signs, standing like mental fences, only accessible to the caretakers who worked in shifts and then left to be with their friends and families.

Danni hung her coat on a peg by the nurses' station and went about her diagnostic routines. Farther down the hall there was a really tall man wearing a flashy cowboy hat and wheeling a gurney. Danni could see that the patient was an adult male. With all her professional training, Danni could quickly identify his wavering consciousness. An occasional outburst of incoherent vocalization suggested that he would soon be awakening. He also seemed to be in pain and was reacting primitively to the large cast that encased his left leg.

"Scuse me Ma'am Docter, dis here guy needs ta be takin down to da windo an yer carcass is in da way. Yu understan it's a mighty good lookin carcass, but it stil needs ta move 'cause dis here guy is kinda startin to make noises an dey figer dat som stimalasion wil halp." Danni didn't know who this character was, but moved so the pair could get by.

The young man on the gurney had probably driven his motorcycle too carelessly or wrecked his snowmobile against a tree. Maybe a horse had caused the man's brain injury. Danni crossed out the horse conjecture. The man was too severely brain damaged for most horse accidents. Besides, he was a big strong-looking specimen, not vulnerable to small bumps and bruises that characterize most horse injuries. Danni's flashing thoughts, however, had activated her concern for Jack. She often worried about Jack. Working all alone on his North Dakota ranch, there would be no one to rescue him in case of a bad accident.

Danni Penfield looked more closely at the unconscious patient's mangled left leg. His face wasn't visible. As with other patients, she'd probably be called in to perform a miracle cure when he started to wake up.

Danni's objective and somewhat cynical attitude was understandable given her upbringing. She had loved this one North Dakota cowboy who played football at Nebraska, but another man she also loved terminated her relationship with The Dakota Colt. She now realized that the only major flaw in her personality was directly related to her codependent relationship with her father who had never accepted Jack as a worthy suitor.

Danni knew Jack's flaw. He had only one. His left knee. Smashed in a football wreck that Danni experienced vicariously in a picture from the Lincoln Herald Times, she had witnessed Jack's undoing. Sometimes she also thought that Jack had one more flaw that really wasn't a personality trait, but just a mistake in judgment. She could never reason away his lack of pursuit. Why hadn't he just demanded that Jack Steele and Danni Penfield join together forever? To hell with what her father wanted.

Danni's last thought that included profanity startled her so much that she bumped into the moving gurney. Luckily the unconscious man was facing away from her and wasn't further injured when she bumped his left knee. She noticed scrawled writing on the patient's cast and old scars around his knee from reconstructive surgery. "Excuse me." Danni looked up at the really tall guy whose brand new cowboy hat was being pushed back by one hand as he propped the other on his hip.

"Ma'am Docter yu seem ta be kinda havin a bad time of it. If'n yud lik ta cum down ta da windo wid us mabe I could giv yu som therpy too. I got lots a time ya understand cause I gots ta sta wid dis sleepin cowpoke." The really tall guy seemed like a real card and Danni reasoned that he was the kind of person that could get by with saying anything to almost anyone.

Danni's mood was suddenly changed since she liked the down home kind of language the really tall guy used. She reflected his invitation. "I ain't got time rite now. But maybe next week we can git together."

Her lingo wasn't completely imitative, but it seemed to amuse the gurney-pushing cowboy. The unconscious patient seemed to stir at the sound of her voice. Danni thought his guttural noises sounded similar to snoring sounds made by Jack in a far away North Dakota bedroom.

The patient's vocalizations snapped her mind back to her father's conflict with Jack. Dr. Penfield never thought anyone was good enough for his only daughter. At the time she was with Jack, Danni still thought she loved her father. Now she wasn't sure if she did or not.

Danni's father, Dr. George Penfield, was a hard driving self-made man with a type "A" personality. He was born on a Nebraska ranch that bordered the North Platte River where Danni's grandfather practiced "horse doctor" medicine. Higher education made an escape from the ranch possible, and blended with native intelligence, he earned a sheepskin with no sheep attached. Years of medical training allowed him to cut chunks of intelligence, personality and speech from his patients' brains in order to save their lives.

He wished for a boy before Danni's birth. George and Mary Penfield had decided to name their child either Danni or Danny depending on the child's sex. That way, even a girl would have a masculine sounding name and could possibly share the outdoors and other father-son activities included in Dr. Penfield's early retirement plans.

When Danni was born, Dr. Penfield was already 43 years old. Being a medical person he knew of all the possible things that could go awry, but only his wildest imagination and short probability allowed him to foresee the cerebral aneurysm that burst and flooded his wife's brain. Heroic surgery was not even attempted because the brain swelling could not be controlled with the most aggressive medication. Standing beside her hospital bed in the intensive care unit, he wondered out loud in words that could not be heard by the baby girl's unconscious mother. "Maybe we waited too long to have our only child and what's going to happen to little Danni when you're gone?"

Two days after Danni's birth, her mother, Mary, died.

In the years that followed, Danni was the pivotal point of every activity in her father's existence. His work took second place to his daughter and he promised himself every day that Danni Penfield would become the best person that could be raised by one man—and two grandparents.

But Danni's behavioral tendencies followed her grandpa's family tree. By the time she was in kindergarten, Danni had visited her grandfather's retirement ranchette near Lincoln, Nebraska more than her little fingers and toes could count.

Danni galloped and "yahooed" toward the barn in a youth-sized, 13-inch Western saddle. Grandpa Jacob laughed at her antics and encouraged her to ride roughhouse on his range bred Appaloosas. By the time she was in fourth grade, she could ride anything that wasn't a complete outlaw. Sometimes, when the chores were done, Grandma and Grandpa would drive their Ford pickup to town.

Seated between them and bouncing on the crackling vinyl, Danni never asked "When are we going to get there" because she knew every landmark that led to the little town with the name she had just plain learned to love. She thought of Crete, Nebraska as her own town and when the three-some hit main street, she could choose to go shopping with Grandma Pearl or go to the restaurant with Grandpa Jacob. Most of the time she went with Grandpa who always sat by the counter on the spinable stools and ordered, "Coffee and a couple a plain doughnuts and give Danni a big glass of milk and one a those white ones." Powdered sugar from her doughnut sprinkled the ruffles on her new dress as she spun round and round and from side to side. Her grandparents had become the mother she had never known.

Every winter Danni returned home to Evanston, Illinois where she rode English style at the riding academy, but every summer she rode at Grandpa's toy ranch. Her tomboyishness became a lifestyle in which internal desires were sublimated. Her psychic energy was vented through horses and athletics.

As she grew older, Danni was always a little insecure about her looks. She had the hard-body look of an over-sized gymnast with broad shoulders, narrow waist and strong thighs. Danni thought she looked a little too masculine. On one occasion, a store clerk had asked, "May I help you sir?" At that point she decided that maybe she was dressing too much like a guy.

Danni's girlfriends were quick to point out that one hundred twenty-five pounds of five-foot seven femininity gets guys' attention. With her dark hair pulled back into a ponytail or tucked under her baseball cap, she assumed an anonymous visage and the smell of shavings mixed with horse manure was an anti-aphrodisiac for most men. Besides, she always thought that men didn't like smart women. Danni was left to her fantasies in which men were almost too realistic to be imaginary.

When she became college age, Danni's father tried in vain to discourage her enrollment at Nebraska. He wanted her to choose Northwestern instead, a college close to home that was Big Ten, but had an Ivy League reputation. Danni's love of horses and her attachment to her grandparents, eventually drew her to Nebraska and her agrarian pedigree.

Before Danni enrolled at Nebraska, Dr. George Penfield seldom visited his home state of Nebraska, but after she enrolled, his plans changed. He then planned to retire in Nebraska so he could be personally supportive of Danni's education. But neither Danni nor her father could gaze into the crystal ball that foretold his shortened existence and her fruitful love. Their combined knowledge would have ignored even the most accurate predictions of fortune. Dr. Penfield did not know his heart would fail and Danni never planned on sitting next to a North Dakota cowboy.

Sociology was a snap class—one that all the football players were "required" to take to make certain their grade point averages would be adequate. Danni took Soc to fill a general elective requirement in her Pre-Med program. The large auditorium promised anonymity, but it was difficult to ignore the person sitting in the next seat.

The day Danni sat down beside Jack's cowboy boots, she didn't know anything about the man that filled them. She only wanted a chair—at least that's what her somewhat arrogant attitude suggested. Danni wanted this strange cattle rustler seated next to her to know that she couldn't care less about him.

But the smell of her "Eau de Stall # 5" perfume gave her away. Before class, Danni had visited her grandfather's farm and as always, was required to clean stalls if she wanted to ride. Even the snub she gave Jack seemed a bit superficial compared to the odor. Jack's casual comment about "smelling like home at the ranch," briefly stiffened her phony resolve to remain mute, but when Jack mentioned his horse called Curly, she was more curious than her aloofness could handle.

"You mean to tell me there's a dead horse in the center of your living room floor? And he's got his head still attached? And that he's been in the family for three generations?"

"Yup." Jack responded with a one-word sentence.

The professor's lecture was, for that day, intellectually unattended. Jack continued to spar verbally with Danni about her Thoroughbred horse that lived a luxurious existence at Grandpa's farm. She told him that he was just jealous and furthermore, any self-respecting horse person wouldn't ride a Dakota broomtail.

That afternoon they made a spontaneous trip to see Danni's horse. Jack didn't have any wheels so they used Danni's little Ford Ranger and even the truck knew they weren't on a mission to see her horse. But all three pretended well. As the two people talked horses, the truck dodged the last driveway puddle.

Jack really made a hit with Danni's grandfather. Swinging her jumping saddle over the big gelding's loins, she slid the saddle forward into position. Danni tried to pretend that she wasn't listening to the male conversation. As Danni rode, her horse's breathing rendered the men's conversation unintelligible. Their voices provided a soothing backdrop for her demonstration.

Although separated in age by over a half-century, the two men agreed on almost every word of every phrase. Her grandfather, having been raised like Jack, could identify with ranch rough. A pleasant camaraderie encircled the group. Her horse, like the centerpiece of an artistic display, floated gracefully through motions that looked like equine ballet. Danni directed the dressage movements with subtlety. Her hands tickled the horse's mouth through three feet of reins as she signaled gait changes, side passes and Lipizzaner action. Their togetherness and unity of motion gave Jack the impression that the powerfully athletic gelding was gliding with his mounted companion simply directing living muscle to greater performance.

Jack's eyes followed every movement of the pair. He turned

to Grandpa and said, "You sure can't see no daylight between Danni and that horse."

The horse's exhalations curled into the crisp autumn Nebraska air and Danni pulled the huge Thoroughbred to a halt. Patting him alongside the neck, she looked to the two men for some sign of approval. They smiled. Jack's facial expression allowed Danni a brief look into a private spot in his brain. She already imagined it to be reserved just for her. It was.

The conversation between Danni and Jack on the way back to the Big Red University intensified. Jack still talked a lot and she was flattered by his attention. Despite her academic superiority and athletic talent, she couldn't believe that a Nebraska football jock could be interested in getting to know her. As her little truck pulled into the field house parking lot, Danni knew for certain that she didn't want Jack to leave for football practice. They sat until the last possible moment to discuss their common bond—horses. Then Jack loped away toward the locker room. But the gloves he had been wearing remained on the truck seat. She'd have to call him tonight.

Danni hurried to her dormitory room. Within minutes she was talking to her father. She wanted to tell him about Jack, but wasn't confident of his reaction. The next best thing was to talk about her grandfather, who reminded her so much of Jack. She thought that Grandpa Jacob must have been just like Jack when he was young. She only mentioned that a friend had gone to the farm to see her horse. Never having had a serious boyfriend, Daddy would never think her companion was male. Dr. Penfield told his daughter for the zillionth time that he loved her and for only the hundredth time, since enrolling at Nebraska, to study hard. He never mentioned the pain deep in his chest.

Danni stood silently beside the phone. The conflict was too terrible. After only knowing Jack for hours, Danni already felt torn between her love at first sight emotions for Jack and her timeless devotion to her father. Danni wished she had informed her loving father about the new attraction in her life. She made it through nine numbers of the redial before returning the phone to its hook.

Danni would have to wait for two hours and forty-five minutes, approximately, for Jack to return to his dorm room. She had to think of a reason to contact the first man that had ever stirred her stomach until the reasoning left her brain. It was simple. She had to call Jack so his hands wouldn't get cold. He needed his gloves. She rationalized that Jack had forgotten them on purpose so that she would contact him later. That really sounded stupid when she self-talked. Of course, there was Sociology too. Finally, she just called him on the horse-talk pretense.

She liked the way Jack's deep masculine voice sounded on the phone. Forever afterwards, his vibrating larynx was imprinted in the deepest part of her brain. She could not forget, delete or repress his male vocalizations. Within a half-hour, they were together in the lobby of Jack's dormitory. Making the scenario even more ridiculous was the fact that Danni forgot to bring the gloves. So enamored was Danni that she could scarcely talk. Jack's voice did the communicating for both of them. Its melodious tones made Danni feel warm and womanly inside. Her knees were weak.

Jack invited Danni to see his dorm room. On his desk were three pictures neatly arranged in a semi-circle. "Are these photos of your mom and dad?" Danni turned toward Jack to see the welling of tears in his eyes.

"Yup, those pictures were taken by a photographer from *Appaloosa News* back about fifteen years ago. I guess you don't know about my mom and dad. I don't have parents anymore. They were killed in a car accident. That was two years ago last February. I had just turned seventeen and we had a great party on my golden birthday, just the day before." Jack stopped trying to say words that would choke.

Danni stood quietly. Having experienced a life-long absence of her mother, Danni hurt for Jack. She reached for Jack and put both arms around his chest staying within the limits their clothes would permit. There was nothing to say.

Jack found it a little easier to talk about the third picture, "And the other picture is one taken of Illusion, our Appaloosa stallion, when he was featured as "Horse of the West" in the Harvey, North Dakota newspaper. It's called *The Herald-Times*. He was really a great horse and he sired colts that were spittin' images. My dad was really attached to him, both emotionally and financially. Illusion was just a nice horse and he also saved our ranch from bankruptcy."

Recognizing Jack's unwillingness to talk further about his parents, Danni tried to be positive. "Illusion is really a gorgeous horse. I'd like to see him some day."

"I don't think that'll be possible. Not that you can't see him, but you can't see him in the flesh. He died two winters ago just after the accident......" Jack's voice started to weaken for the second time.

"I'd love to see your ranch sometime. It reminds me of the stories that Grandpa used to tell about western Nebraska. You remind me so much of him." Danni tried to smother herself in the opening of Jack's shirt.

Jack's bulging chest muscles flexed against Danni's face. She could feel the heat of embarrassment rising on her cheeks and turned away to walk toward the door. Jack reached out and grabbed Danni's arm to restrain her movement. She couldn't move—not just because of his strength, but because of her weakness. "You don't have to leave yet do you?" Jack's question was strictly rhetorical.

Looking at the floor because she was afraid to see the expression in Jack's eyes, Danni shook her head sideways. It was hard for her to talk because she wanted desperately to say things that she had only seen lovers say in movies. She had never said those intimate phrases to anyone and would be afraid to use the words that were circling her lower brain. Besides, it was too soon. Sometimes silence is better than words.

After what seemed like several minutes, but was actually only seconds, Danni glanced upward. Jack's eyes were fixed. The pupils of his large eyes were dilated. Danni diverted her gaze because Jack might see what she was really feeling. The racing of her heart might show more than the blushing of her face. Jack broke the silence awkwardly, sharply squeezing Danni's hand to lead her out the door. There was stillness in the night air. Jack's mouth searched for the warmth of Danni's lips and when they were his, Danni pressed against the hardness of Jack's body. Then the darkness of the chilled night air consumed their images.

Danni was awake at 5:00 A.M. After eating lightly and fixing her hair with greater care than ever before, she dressed in a casual jogging suit and walked briskly to class making certain to sit in the identical seat as the lecture before. After all, the Sociology professor wanted to know the exact location of all 300 students. By 7:50, her chair in the large auditorium was occupied and when Jack didn't show until his usual time, which was exactly when class started, Danni started to wonder if he would show at all.

In usual form, Jack arrived just as the professor was beginning his lecture. Jack's angular frame weaved through already seated students to get the **"saved"** chair beside Danni. His Wrangler jeans, clearly outlining his masculine lower extremities, brushed lightly on Danni's jogging attire as he bounced on one leg between her legs and with one motion, spun, and dropped his six-one, two hundred pound wide receiver frame into the cushioned seat. "Thanks for saving me a place. I always like to sit next to the best looking woman in the crowd. Your hair is really pretty."

The lecture was more boring than usual. But the camaraderie was great.

Days passed into weeks and then into months and as the days shortened, the sun shifted from north to south. Multicolored leaves crunched as footballs filled the stadium air. With Jack on the Cornhusker roster as a freshman wide receiver, Danni found it necessary to deviate from her Pre-Med studies. Bundled in blankets that were inside sleeping bags, Danni and her girlfriends watched as the Dakota Colt brought ooo's and ahhh's from the fans.

Her chest would almost burst with pride as Jack was introduced before each game. As his long galloping stride carried his muscles and sinew over the manicured grass, she wanted to possess every pound of his flesh.

When Jack lay motionless on the turf she screamed and was unable to choke out even the first word. Her trachea swelled with tears that overflowed from her eyes. It was impossible for Danni to see the football field. She rushed from the stadium to be with her man whose stillness on the stretcher strengthened her vow to become a rehab doctor. Dr. Danni Penfield and the miracles of modern medicine would someday rescue traumatically brain-injured people. Quietly she took another vow—to never leave Jack's side.

At the hospital, the assistant coach explained that Jack had "just got his bell rung," that "he'd be OK" and "he's been asking for you." Danni smiled back the tears. Jack didn't need to feel any worse. Danni steadied The Colt as they sat bedside, consuming treats and providing mutual entertainment. Jack wanted to know what had happened that made him lose his memory. Danni explained that, after making a reception, a linebacker had tackled him, catching him on his blindside.

Jack was full of questions. "But did I hang on to the ball? Did we win the game? What was the score?"

Danni, pretending to be taking an exam said, "Yes, all of the above."

The next Saturday, Jack caught two touchdown passes and the wide receiver coach joked, "Maybe that thumpin' you took woke you up rather than put you to sleep and by the way, who was that pretty girl that came to see you at the hospital?"

Their togetherness was as natural as the shifting seasons. Snowfall, that seems to spell dormancy to the earth, covers newly seeded plants so they may later flourish. And so, secretly grew their affections. Danni only told her closest girlfriends and confided with her grandfather. "I really like Jack's unassuming attitude. He's not like most guys who strut their stuff on the outside, like a peacock when you first meet them, and later find there's a turkey underneath. He reminds me of you, Grandpa. I bet you were like Jack when you were his age."

"Well, I guess that's true to a certain extent. But I never had the ability that Jack shows. You know Danni, it's even more remarkable that Jack is the way he is when he gets all the attention he does." Grandpa spoke with wisdom.

"Most men have such plastic exteriors. But Jack doesn't. He's really captured the heart I didn't know I had. He's got an inner beauty that goes way beyond his handsomeness and strength. He seems like a rose that's inside a case. Under the glass the softness of the petals and the fragrance of the flower are still protected by thorns. But Grandpa, I want to get inside the glass case and around those thorns. I want to shatter the glass and get just one whiff of the rose. Maybe someday I can wear the pretty flower in my hair." Danni smiled shyly, realizing that she had just gushed emotions at Grandpa's willing ear.

"Does your dad know you feel this way?" Grandpa's question seemed abrupt and hurtful.

"Not yet. But I plan on telling him pretty soon." Danni stopped talking about Jack, but her thinking of him continued.

Danni wanted to tell Dad about her feelings for Jack. But she was afraid of her father's reaction. Dr. George Penfield wanted his daughter to reach her full potential and he saw to it that Danni had every opportunity to do so. His stern, but loving, approach to child rearing made Danni the wonder woman she was. Nothing was too good for her and he spared neither word nor deed to make her a disciplined, but caring person.

Without being fully aware of his own intentions, Dr. Penfield was trying, to the extent a father could try, to create Danni in his own image. Dr. Penfield and his daughter had planned their future together. He would retire at the ripe young age of 60 and they would be able to spend lots of time exploring both the outdoors and Danni's medical training. The burden of single-handedly raising his daughter had distorted his perspective and stressed his failing heart.

Danni felt conflict between loyalty to her father and desire for Jack. She knew her father would never approve of her feelings and at times, she felt like chucking the whole education bit and moving to North Dakota. Jack's persuasive personality and cowboy charm didn't help.

Jack had written Danni a note in which he requested the honor of her presence at the next Sociology extra-credit film.

Popcorn, coated with butter and sprinkled with salt, tasted better than anything from Danni's dorm room popper. Jack's arrival with two paper glasses filled with soda made the cheap college treat taste even better. Sagging seats covered with chewed red velvet had served the auditorium well for the last fifty years. Every cushioned seat was taken. Even the first two rows that tilted heads into stiff necks were stuffed shoulder to shoulder and standing room only students waited with anticipation.

All Sociology classes had been dismissed and attendance had, therefore, been required of all students. The nature of the featured movie, however, did not require role taking or that buttered popcorn be provided. Featuring provocative content related to pornography, the advertisements and newspaper inserts had aroused students' curiosity.

By now, Jack and Danni had become Sociology soul mates and as the movie began, Jack's hand searched the tub bottom to find one last unpopped kernel. His thumb and forefinger carried it to Danni's lips, "Don't you become an old maid like this."

Danni expelled the seed into the center of her palm and grasping Jack's left hand, pressed the lonely kernel between their hands, "You might have something to say about that." Pressing the lifeline of her palm into pain, the kernel adhered to a notch in Danni's hand. She pushed hard against Jack's hand to make the pain of the indentation more intense. It was like the masochistic enjoyment of mild pain just before pleasure. Soon the nerve endings would stop sending and that small piece of skin would be numb. Then, she could convert numbness into permanent pleasure. Danni knew that the pain must be of equal intensity to Jack and she was determined not to give in before he did.

"You're one tough cookie." Jack released Danni's hand and with complete acceptance and gentleness placed the hurt against the cheek of his face. Danni knew for certain that one of Jack's most admirable qualities was his ability to be simultaneously tough and gentle. She recognized her need for both gentle affection and unthrottled passion.

There was laughter and hushed silence as college students, embarrassed by the film's content, tried to reconcile their internal beliefs with what they had just seen on screen. Danni squirmed uneasily, and Jack's hand pulled away from her hand as the content got particularly racy. They were both thinking. For only seconds, their mutual self-consciousness separated rubbing shoulders and tangled hands. Then, the magnets that were Danni and Jack slid back to mid-line where only the armrest could interfere.

"Next time we'll have to go to a real movie—not just some professor's porno assignment." Jack joked as they exited the crowded auditorium.

"Let's go to Crete next weekend and see the Sunday afternoon matinee. It'll be a good neutralizer for the stuff we saw today." Danni poked Jack's ribs with her fist as he made a side-passing movement wedging her wrist snuggly between his upper arm and ribcage.

"There's no reason we can't celebrate right now even if this wasn't a real movie. I know a place outside of town that's got the greatest strawberry malts. They use real strawberries and one malt is big enough for two starving college students like us." Danni knew Jack's offer was legitimate, although she would not be assured of half the malt, because of Jack's voracious appetite. "If we go right now I can still get back in time for football practice."

Danni was intrigued by the hole-in-the-wall, restaurant that Jack had chosen. A large buffalo head hung above the full-length glass mirror that reflected the images of patrons on revolving stools. Seated with elbows on a mahogany bar they turned faces in unison, "Hi Colt, how ya doin?"

"Hi guys, I want you to meet Danni Penfield. She's from Chicago or someplace close by, so I want you to behave yourselves. She's from the upper crust of society. Her dad operates on brains and she's going to be a rehab doctor—one that works with patients after strokes and head injury."

Jack wanted every single one of his cowboy friends to know that he was proud to be with her.

"These malts really are big. And look at those saddles. How old are they anyway? I've never seen anything like that before." Danni was studying the collection of highback saddles that decorated the stairway railing.

"Aren't they great? You know I've got a saddle like that at home. My grandpa, Joe Steele, got it from a saddle maker in Colorado way back in the 1920's." A somber visage consumed Jack's face and Danni knew without asking that the time had come for Jack to talk about the ROCKING J.

Danni listened sincerely as stories of cattle and horses colored the saloon air. Uncle John and Illusion were still at the ranch. James and Annie Steele were no longer there. Jack wanted to return to the ranch. As she slurped the last few drops of strawberry up the straw, there was one thing that Danni knew for sure. Jack was the most fascinating person she had ever known. Exceeding his physical prowess were the depths of his personality and genealogy. Someday she would live with Jack in his North Dakota memory.

There was still time enough for more afternoon pleasure. They returned to Danni's dorm room.

A steadily beating heart changed from 130 to 90 to 70 and leveled off at 60 beats per minute. Danni's ear lay resting on the pectoralis major muscle of Jack's chest. She already knew the origin, insertion and innervation of most large muscles and in a few years would capitalize on this advanced knowledge. Danni knew that Jack had the heart of a true sprinter, one could ascend rapidly and lie quiet quickly. His forever state brought on by the petite mort of love's relaxation, seemed what the French expression meant literally—"the little death."

Danni's head rose and fell with the deep breathing that was less than half his heart rate. She wondered about the capacity of Jack's emotional heart, which she knew was physically titanic. Watching his eyes flicker open, she brushed his forehead with her fingers and returned his eyelids to a closed position as she said, "You've got 19 more minutes to sleep before you have to go to football practice." She watched the deep breathing contractions of Jack's chest and listened to his snoring. She had to own this man. Her father would just have to accept Jack as the other man of her heart.

After discussing her plans with Jack, Danni decided to arrange a Jack-George meeting. She knew that her father's heart was failing and that stress of any kind could be fatal. But for her own peace of mind, Danni needed to reconcile her father's unrealistic expectations with the plans she had made for her future with Jack. Danni made a decision. In order to bring the two men together, she would invite her father to a Nebraska football game. Jack knew about Dr. Penfield's visit, but George didn't know about the Colt.

The Dakota Colt was especially spectacular that day. Maybe it was because, for the first time since tenth grade, he felt he had a parent watching. After one galloping catch in the end zone, Danni's father commented on the outstanding play of the man the Big Red football program listed as six-one and two hundred pounds. The nickname **"DAKOTA COLT"** in bold capital letters under his program photo caught Dr. Penfield's attention. "What a name! I bet he's a wild one."

Seizing that opportunity and before her father could insert any further derogatory remarks, Danni blurted out what she had been trying to tell her father for nearly three months: "I know Dakota. His real name is Jack and I invited him to Grandpa's place for supper."

Nebraska won again and the meal that Danni's 78 year- old Grandma Pearl prepared was another victory. In her sweet way, and always wanting to encourage such things, Danni's grandma had seated Jack and Danni next to each other. With years of diagnostic experience, Dr. Penfield began sizing up his competition and Jack never thought there was any.

Dr. George Penfield, on a restrictive heart diet, grumbled as he cursed the meat that never reached his plate.

With a full stomach, Grandpa Jacob pushed his chair away from the table. With a smile and wink he grabbed his windbreaker, "I've got a few barn chores, but I don't need any help. If I don't show up in a half hour come looking for me."

"Would you two go watch TV so Grandma and I can clean up the kitchen? Unless you want to help........."Danni shooed the other two men to the living room.

Jack knew that Dr. Penfield was a neurosurgeon and tried to establish rapport by talking about his "bell ringing" concussion. And George, as he instructed Jack to call him, told of his youth on the North Platte River. Danni smiled into her grandma's twinkling eyes as she heard the male voices from the next room break into legato. Grandma gave Danni a big hug and said, "Everything will work out fine."

There was too much noise in the kitchen to eavesdrop on the living room conversation. Two of the three men Danni loved most in the whole world were talking and she wanted to discreetly listen to their continuous vocalizations. Danni turned the dishwasher off. Besides, Grandpa would soon be in from doing chores and didn't like the noise.

A week later Danni received a personal letter from her father. The message was clear and expected. He thought Jack was really a nice guy, **BUT** not right for her. Danni wondered if her father would ever approve of anyone.

To make matters even worse, Jack had invited Danni to his ranch during semester break.

ROCKING J

By semester break, Jack had peaked Danni's curiosity about his ranch life. He proposed that they travel to North Dakota in her pickup and Jack volunteered to drive. After failing to reach her father by phone, Danni decided to write a letter in which she described the depth of her relationship with Jack and her upcoming trip to the ROCKING J. Danni simply, and innocently, wanted her father to know her whereabouts since she had always made a practice of doing so. She also wanted to be honest with her father about the importance of Jack in her recent life.

Jack was surprised that Danni traveled so well. The miles wore down. They passed snow-covered wheat fields and soon the water tower of Harvey, North Dakota came into view. Located in the center of the state on Highway 52, Harvey had been Jack's home since birth. As Danni crowded closer to Jack on the Ranger's vinyl seat, he turned toward a sign suspended on a cable between two second-hand creosote-blackened telephone poles. Driving under the sign, Danni quietly mouthed the letters: R-O-C-K-I-N-G J. A permanent brand was burned into her brain. Jack was home. And Danni was with him.

Jack's four months of verbal descriptions were now authenticated. Danni could see rusty barbed wire as it sagged between posts that were no longer straight with the world. The driveway was full of potholes and all the buildings needed repair and paint. A drooping clothesline nearly reached the ground despite the absent weight of wet Wranglers. Gray weathered corral planks surrounded a few hundred-head of cattle and a smaller bunch of horses. As Danni's little pickup neared the house, an old dog, limping on one front foot, tried to bark them away. Then, he saw Jack and his tail wagged.

Scenes from Harvey, North Dakota

*Welcoming sign to
Harvey, North Dakota*

*Water tower in
Harvey, North Dakota*

Grain elevator at Harvey, North Dakota

The football season was over and Jack needed a return to ranch life. He knew everything was perfect. The six yearling colts he had come home to help Uncle John break were standing on the right side of the fence with steam pouring out their nostrils.

Snow covered the North Dakota landscape. The partially abandoned ranch, that Jack inherited when his parents died, stood like a permanent Dakota Christmas card that would always say, **"welcome home."**

When he had been in high school, winter mornings meant feeding the steers before breakfast and a twenty-mile school bus ride. After school, depending on the season, there was either football or basketball practice followed by a ride home in the coach's car and then even more night chores. Sandwiched between were Algebra, History and English. The week's highlights always included Friday night games in which Jack's hardened existence was melded with raw talent and at best, good high school coaching. Running fast and catching the pigskin were not even second nature to Jack, they were Jack.

Jack had tried to explain his Spartan upbringing to Danni. She could vicariously understand because of her grandfather's stories of ranch life. Grandpa had grown up on a cattle ranch in Western Nebraska. Later, when he retired to a small ranchette near Crete, Nebraska, Danni's summertime memories were crammed with an old man's nostalgic reminiscences of branding, bucking and bulldogging.

As Jack and Danni walked up the weathered steps of the ranch house, she was beginning to fully understand the circumstances of Jack's upbringing.

"What is that thing?" Danni had noticed the black and white spotted Appaloosa hide, hanging on the wall of the ranch house mud room.

Jack didn't tell the story that only Uncle John and he knew and dragged a "red herring" across the conversation to distract her from the real issue. "I guess lots of people think it's funny to have a horse in the house. But this one don't eat and we don't have to clean up after him either."

Danni knew there was more to the story, but decided to wait until Jack was ready to explain.

Uncle John, who had lived on the ROCKING J his entire life, greeted Jack with a callused handshake. "I got supper on the cookstove if you kids are hungry."

Mashed potatoes, boiled within red skins, were scooped directly from kettle to plate and the simmering venison steak from frying pan to their side. The old dog, Pal, was parked next to the table in hopes of snarfing discarded food scraps. The bare wood floor showed some varnish marks in less traveled areas of the large kitchen. Except for scratch marks, the floor was completely smooth around the rectangular oak table. According to bachelor standards, the house was well kept and only a few remnants of femininity remained.

Jack's parents, tragically killed while driving home from one of Jack's sophomore basketball games, had tried to make the small North Dakota Ranch profitable. Their daylight to dark work schedule was interrupted only to see that their young and coltish son had learned well to read, write and cipher. In 8th grade, the football coach discovered that the straggly teenager could outrun anyone on the high school team. Jack's mom and dad couldn't wait to see their only child dressed like a Trojan warrior in his first football uniform. He was their one escape from ranch work.

The ROCKING J was always home to Jack even though its acreage was smaller than what he knew as a teenager. His father's R. T. Frazier highback saddle remained on the stairway railing as it had since Jim Steele moved from Montana to North Dakota. Without even asking if she wanted to know, Jack told Danni the family story of **"The Saddle."**

When Jack's mother, Annie, became engaged she didn't know that she would also marry the ROCKING J. At first she couldn't understand why her husband needed to keep a saddle in the house. After James Steele traced the saddle's history, Jack's mother not only left it peacefully on the railing, but also regularly dusted and polished the family heirloom. The saddle maker, Robert Thompson Frazier, had owned a saddlery in Pueblo, Colorado. After fighting in the Civil War, Frazier's father taught him how to make the best saddles in the West. For a while he lived in Leadville, and presumably to get his saddle business started, moonlighted as deputy sheriff. In 1881 he joined another saddle maker named Gallup and in 1898 bought out Gallup and Frazier to become the R. T. Frazier Saddlery. The shop kept going for fourteen years after Mr. Frazier died.

Jack's grandpa, Joseph Steele, had known Mr. Frazier. Respectfully, Jack called him Mr. In 1920, the Frazier saddle had been acquired on a horse trade. Grandpa had swapped a horse worth about two hundred dollars for a new Frazier saddle.

Grandpa Joe had patiently told his grandson about all eight stamps on the saddle. Some were large and others small. Some said "Pueblo" and others said "Pueblo, Colo." One

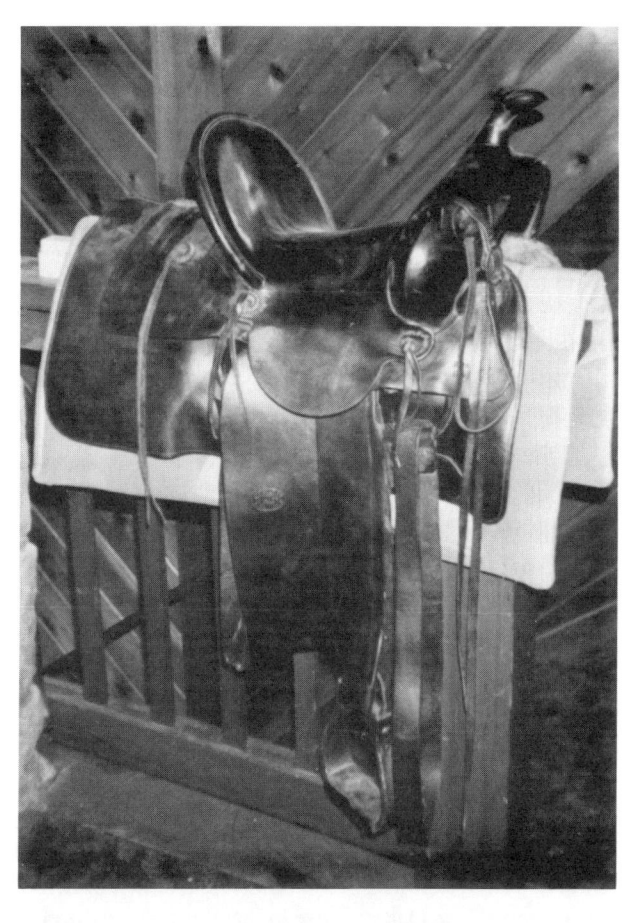

Robert Thompson Frazier highback saddle, acquired by Jack's grandfather on a horse trade

stamp even said "R. T. Frazier trademark." But they all said "Frazier."

Grandpa's story about the saddle concluded the same way every time. "That man was proud of his work and he recorded history in the leather. I gave that saddle to your dad and he'll give it to you and down the line."

Jack showed the largest saddle stamp to Danni and as her hand traced the indentations she knew that someday her children would know the story she had just heard. Covertly, she hid a secret message of that Dakota encounter in her memory. Shamelessly, Danni reached for Jack's hand and forced it upon the stamped depression she had just traced.

Jack's eyes explored Danni's face. Then, he turned his vision inward to check his own mind. He had to be certain that she could tolerate more family secrets. Truth costs.

Jack explained to Danni why the place looked so run-down. "After my folks were killed, there were a lot of bad things that happened and the ROCKING J almost went under. The bank was ready to foreclose and we were faced with losing the ROCKING J. So, we sold most of the ranch to the neighbors."

Only a few hundred acres of the original Rocking J remained intact. Three hundred brood cows and a mixed bunch of horses fed off the Dakota range in the summer and the one-cutting grass hay during the winter. The farm chores kept Uncle John's calendar filled and Jack's semester vacation provided his weary uncle a welcome work relief. Wear and tear was showing on the old man's lined face and he had a stooped walk with shortened steps. Jack had watched Uncle

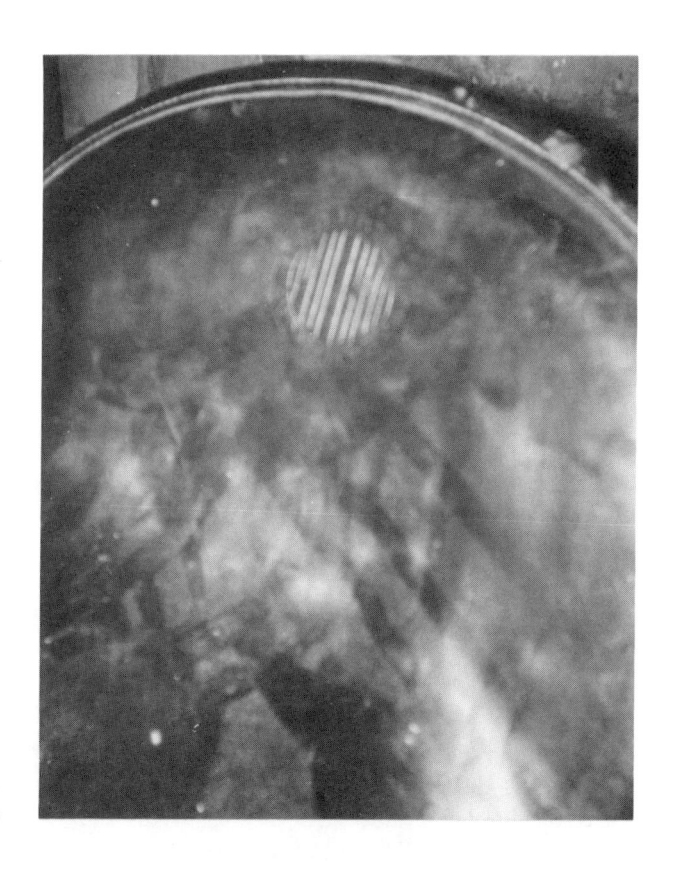

*Largest stamp on the
R. T. FRAZIER highback saddle*

John grow old and wondered how much longer he would be able to manage the ROCKING J.

Danni looked out the window and could see blown snow curling into a drift. A winter storm, fully brewed in the Rockies, would soon invade the barren Dakota prairies. She noticed the brood cows huddled together against the wind and wondered why they faced the driving snow. Jack explained that, unlike horses, cattle face the wind in storms. Horses turn their tails to the wind.

There was peacefulness inside the ranch house that transcended the Godforsakenness just outside. As darkness invaded, Jack's uncle, in long underwear and insulated coveralls, made his way to the barn. Jack quickly joined him and on the way out the door, told Danni to take care of the house while they did chores. Darkness came.

Slashing snow made the swaying yard light barely visible, creating a mirage of twisted and pulsating light. Danni wondered if the men had survived their walk to the barn since they had been gone for nearly two hours. She was relieved to hear the stomping of boots in the porch and greeted Jack with a welcoming smile. Then she kissed his face, not so much as a display of affection, but because she wanted to sense his body's winter vitality. Both of Danni's arms could not reach all the way around her man who was packed in longjohns and snowmobile gear. Jack jokingly rubbed his cold cheeks against the tender skin of Danni's neck and as she recoiled from the shock, Jack told her, "This is just a little storm. Just wait till she really gets wound up."

Although Danni wasn't finished cleaning, the house was neater than it had been for years. It had known a woman's touch. Even though Danni was a tough tomboy, she was still female and knew instinctively about gathering and nesting. The contrast between bachelor and homemaker were apparent since Danni had only completed part of the cleaning. Rather than just sweeping the dirt under a convenient rug, Danni had also dusted. She had so stirred the dust that, at one point, Danni had to go outside the house for a breath of air. The ROCKING J vacuum cleaner had become extinct and was replaced with a large bristled broom. Danni had adaptively regressed to the before-electricity system and matter-of-factly swept the living room carpet. Uncle John's comment made her feel appreciated. "Jack, I didn't realize you knew somebody that was both good looking and ambitious."

"I tried to clean the living room, but didn't know what to do about Curly. I remember you telling me about him when we first met in Sociology. I stayed away from him with the broom." Danni sounded almost afraid.

"Some people have bear rugs on their living room or den floor, but we're ranchers, so we keep Curly there to remind people that this place is the ROCKING J. He was Grandpa's favorite horse and was pretty valuable to top it off. He was a Baskir Curly. Did you notice his curly hair? That permanent wave he's got came from God. Only a few horses have ringlets like that." Jack had already justified Curly's taxidermied existence on the living room floor, but continued to explain.

"One day Grandpa Joe missed Curly at the feedbunk and found him tangled in barbed wire, bleeding to death. Like all good cowboys, he took care of his horse right to the end. He put him out of his misery with his 30-30 rifle. The fatal spot for a horse is squarely between the eyes and exactly three and one-half inches above. You can still see the bullet mark that the taxidermist was told to preserve to constantly remind Grandpa of the pain he felt when he had to shoot old Curly." Even with Curly in Horse Heaven, Jack wasn't through with the story.

Uncle John listened closely to make sure it was told accurately. "You probably thought Roy Rogers was the first to have his horse preserved. Well, that rearing Trigger with stuffing inside ain't got nothin' on old Curly. It was in the dead of winter, so Grandpa Joe skinned out Curly and sent him all the way to Albert Lea, Minnesota to get tanned and backed properly. He told the taxidermist to leave Curly's head on and use false eyes to make him look alive. When Curly came back to Colorado, appearing to almost be ready for another day of ranch work , Grandpa put Curly on the living room floor to surprise his new wife. Grandma had been grocery shopping and when she saw Curly with his eyes looking alive and his ears pointing forward, she screamed and dropped the grocery bags on the floor. "It's a good thing she'd put the sugar sack down in the kichen or Curly would have gotten 10 pounds of loose sugar, not the sugar cubes that Grandpa gave him for rewards." Jack's talk of sugar cubes almost made the forever-somnolent Curly vocalize a begging nicker.

"I guess you don't have to worry about being a little afraid of Curly. Grandma protested a little at first to having him in the house, but she adjusted. So will you, kid." Jack playfully put Danni in a headlock and wrestled her to the living room floor. They landed in a scrambled pile looking directly at Curly's face.

Danni's hands pressed against Jack's cheeks as she lay under his sinewy body. With an unintended, joking spirit, Danni flippantly said, "Most people don't have any horses in their house and you've got two! I guess I'll have to accept Curly because he's been in the family for so long........." Jack

*CURLY, Joe Steel's favorite horse,
made into a life-like horse rug*

interrupted Danni's apology by tickling her ribs, sending her into squirming, giggling contortions. Still laughing, she entered territory where humor was not welcome.

Regarding Illusion, Danni spoke too carelessly, "I guess I'll have to accept Curly, but that ugly horse hide in the porch is beyond my understanding. You are going to have to get rid of him if you want me to live here!"

Jack's entire body stiffened and his smile snapped straight. He said nothing and left the room with Danni still on the floor.

Because of the severity of the storm, Uncle John decided to watch the cattle. Between wind gusts, he could see the huddled cattle. Like a playful child, Danni scraped the frosty etchings on the kitchen window with her fingernails. Turning to the old man, she asked, "Why do you keep watching the cattle?"

Uncle John explained that when the milling of the three hundred or so cows stopped, the snow would soon bury them in a large suffocating snowdrift. They had plenty to eat and were not bothered by the cold temperatures, but danger lurked in the wind.

In severe winter storms, cattle huddle together for protection from the wind. As the drifting snow surrounds them, the cattle smother themselves in a vain effort to survive. The old-time ranchers had invented a way to save the cattle in such storms. By continuous movement, the stomping herd would trample the soft snow into hardened drifts.

"You kids go to bed and get some rest. I'll stay here and watch the storm and call you if it gets too bad." Uncle John, with a stooped walk, made his way to the cookstove to refill the firebox with finely split white oak.

Jack showed Danni to the guestroom. In the room was a steel bed covered with patchwork quilts that descended from Jack's grandmother. A large vanity with an oval shaped mirror stood on the linoleum flooring and handmade scatter rugs, woven from torn rags, lined a pathway from the door to the bed. Before leaving for his room, Jack talked in quiet and serious tones about the blizzard.

He told Danni stories of similar storms in which the ROCKING J crew joined forces to keep the cattle circling for two days. With extreme effort, Jim, John and Jack Steele had saved every cow. A neighbor, new to ranching, didn't realize that his cattle needed to be herded. When the rendering truck could finally reach their dead bodies, two hundred frozen brood cows were winched by hind ankles, making their trip to market as twenty truckloads of mink food.

Jack told Danni that, if the storm grew too intense, she would be responsible for cooking. The house would be cold enough, but the windchill outside would be life threatening. She would have to prepare food like Grandma did when she cooked for the thrashing crew. Danni asked, "What's thrashing?"

Jack first explained that the word should properly be pronounced, "threshing." In the days before combines rolled across the grain fields on pneumatic tires, thrashing rigs did the same job in stationary position. The work of hauling the unthrashed bundles, separating the harvest, piling the straw and hauling the grain required a huge crew that was famished at every feeding. That, explained Jack, was the origin of the phrase, "eating like a thrashing crew."

Danni would also be responsible for stoking fires and drying the work clothes. The life of the ROCKING J would depend on keeping the crew strong, as well as, preventing fatigue and frostbite. Danni understood as well as a city girl could.

As Danni and Jack stood before the vanity mirror, they spoke softly, quietly and intensely. Jack told Danni more about the room furniture, the ranch house and the horses of the ROCKING J. Danni lacked the answer to only one question. "I could tell that you were hurt when I asked about the horse hide in the porch. What's the story behind that spotted horse?"

Jack, with measured and halting speech, told the descriptive parts of the story that were not taboo. "That's a private, family matter and I'd rather keep it that way. Maybe some day I hope to feel the freedom to tell you the whole story. That horse was the salvation of the ROCKING J. I know you want to know more so I'll just tell you his name was Illusion. He was our herd stallion. My dad bought him when he was just a weanling colt and he lived at this ranch until he was nineteen. He threw about 75% colored colts out of almost any kind of mare and over half of them were leopard spotted like him. To top it off most of his babies were black and white. That horse was what made this ranch possible. He kept us from going broke by siring those vividly contrasting hides of living color. He was, to us, like Joseph's Coat of Many Colors. I promise that, when the time is right, you'll know everything that I know about Illusion."

Danni put her arms around Jack. She could sense his remorse over the loss of Illusion. And if the cattle died, the ranch would go under. Jack's hardened muscles tightened

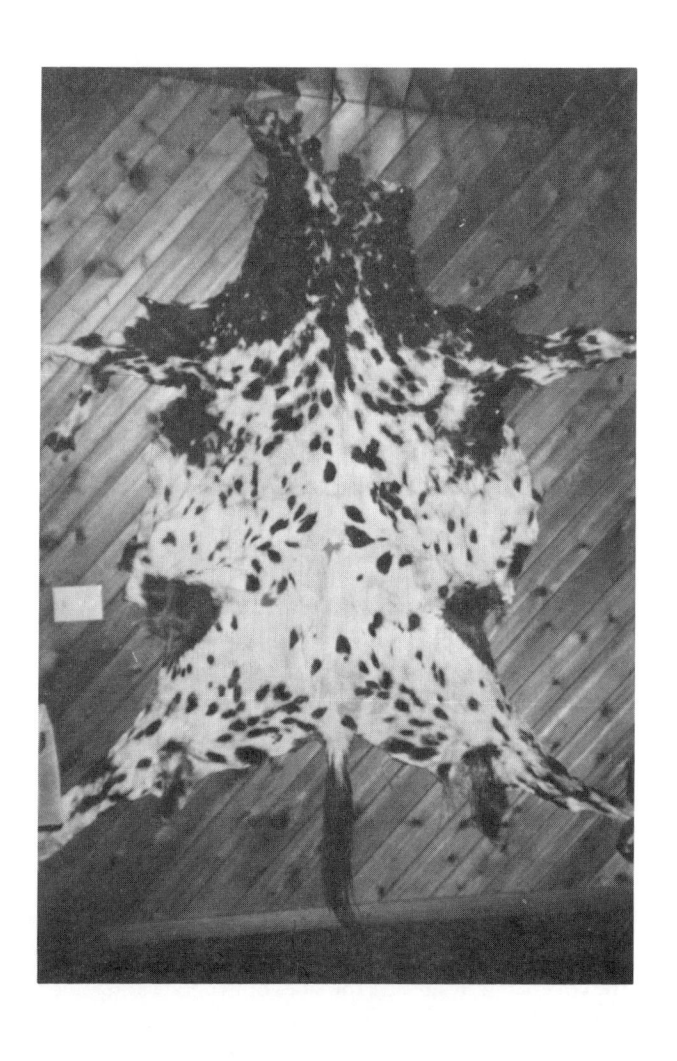

ILLUSION, a horse hide made from the skin of the famous herd sire of the ROCKING J

as he clung to Danni for support. He needed her comfort and reassurance. Linebackers could not compare with nature's ferocity.

As Jack sat on the edge of Danni's bed, his soft whispering came naturally like a beginning wind wisp. He was glad that she was with him. He told her so. He valued her companionship. He told her so. He loved her. He told her so, but she knew that even before his mouth formed the words. Danni hadn't realized that her love for Jack could become deeper. Sometimes storms do that.

Then Jack went to his room. He tried to sleep. Nothing could be gained by worrying about what God was finding hard to prevent. Neither the storm within his chest or outside the window could be stopped. Wind moved the curtain. That was cold and harsh reality.

Unable to sleep, Jack looked out his bedroom window at the quickening blizzard. He wondered if Danni was afraid and with quiet steps made his way to the doorway of the guestroom. Danni had not slept either. Hearing the creaking boards of the ranch house hallway, she whispered above the wind, "Jack, Jack come here. I need another blanket. The wind's coming right through the window."

Jack went back to his room and robbed the largest down-filled quilt. After throwing it over Danni's bed, he tucked the covers tightly around the sides of her body and folded her feet inside the excess length. As he turned to leave, Danni's hand reached out to firmly clasp his wrist. With little resistance Jack relented, falling backwards onto the pile of blankets that surrounded Danni.

A huge wind gust shook the ROCKING J ranch house. Shivering with the chill of winter, Jack looked at the opening in the blankets. Danni's hand was still restraining his departure and her opposite hand raised the blankets as she whispered above the wind, "Crawl inside the covers and warm up. You know you'll have to get up in the middle of the night so you better get that core body temperature up."

The guest room temperature cracked the water filled glass. Danni's arms wrapped all the way around Jack's body. Because of the darkness in the room, Jack hadn't realized that Danni was completely naked. "No wonder you were cold. You need to wear lots of clothes, even at night, when the weather's like this."

Danni's seductive invitation transformed the winter outside the window into a summer breeze, "But Jack I wanted you instead."

Jack forgot about the weather. His callused hands trembled as he crowded Danni's side of the bed. Soft, smooth and delicate, her fingers removed his insulated long underwear top. The hair of his chest brushed her breasts before his muscle tissue descended its weight upon the upper half of her body.

The yard light, swaying from gust to gust, barely shed enough illumination to cast shadows. Before Danni and Jack embraced, they could both see silent mouths that smiled seriously. Their lips met halfway as though compromising desire—neither willing to deny nor confirm their individual needs—but needing beyond their separate entities.

The wind intensified. The wind-chill outside the ranch house dropped to seventy-below zero. Jack's longjohn bottoms were now in the fold he had made for Danni's feet and his entire body lay nakedly aroused. Danni touched Jack lightly over his entire skin's surface. Lifting her buttocks, Jack pulled Danni completely against him. There were no words spoken and except for the breathing of two people and the sound of wind in the Dakota night, the ROCKING J was totally silent.

Then sleep came swiftly.

At midnight, Jack was awakened by a knock on the guest room door. Carefully moving away from Danni so he wouldn't awaken her, he reached for the white porcelain knob. The look on his uncle's face meant only one thing.

Jack quickly got dressed and went back to Danni's bedside—this time trying to alert her. She wondered what was wrong and Jack quickly assured her that nothing was wrong if the proper action was quickly taken. The cattle were beginning to join together to protect themselves from the raging wind and with no shelter they would soon be consumed by the blizzard. It was time to begin the drudgery. The cattle had to be kept moving until the storm subsided.

The work needed to begin immediately and because of the ferocity of the wind, the cattle would only respond to herding from horseback. That meant one thing—get the horses saddled and ride in shifts throughout the night. After putting on all the layers of clothing that would fit beneath coveralls and pulling a facemask stocking cap over his head, Jack jerked his snowmobile boots over two pair of woolen socks.

Danni had never seen anyone dressed so ridiculously and tried not to laugh. Despite Jack's warnings, she did not fully realize how vicious a seventy-below windchill could feel as it penetrates bare skin. In only seconds, exposed human tissue would become frostbitten. Any protection less than total would sacrifice both humans and animals to the storm.

Like soldiers before battle, the two men and one woman planned a strategy. After saddling, Jack would take the first shift for no more than one hour or for as long as he could physically tolerate the cold. Uncle John would take the next hour, and so on, until the storm abated and the cattle could live on their own.

Both men knew more about blizzards than they cared to remember. With silently expressed fear, they shook hands wishing each other good luck and survival. The handshake was an unspoken oath. It was a contract that was better than "a man's word" or a Supreme Court Ruling. Macho attitudes could not be tolerated.

There was only one way to save the cattle and the crew. Old-fashioned blood and guts had to be tempered with sense beyond common. Human fatigue or frostbite meant that the cattle saving operation would cease and when the North Dakota wind died down, the calmness after the storm would be a silent grief of asphyxiation.

A plentiful supply of warm high-energy food would refuel the men's bodies that would struggle against the blizzard. The men needed nutrition, rest and dry clothes. While in the ranch house, their body temperatures had to be elevated to the very core, capturing enough heat to tolerate another hour of frozen hell. Danni would keep the home fires burning.

Danni stood beside Jack and his loyal canine partner, Pal. A two-foot snowdrift had already accumulated on the front porch and when Jack opened the front door, a gust of wind blew snow over the length of the ranch house kitchen. Jack and Pal waded away from the front door. His figure vanished before he reached the swaying yard light that was now only a dim beacon. Jack knew about these storms from childhood and forced his eyes to stay open enough to search for the next marker. The faint light outside the barn grew brighter. After a few more giant steps through deepening snowdrifts, Jack finally reached the barn. To reach the waiting horses, a foot of snow had to be pushed away from the door. Jack applied his muscle, ripping open the bottom half of the split barn door.

Two horses, a bay and a sorrel with Appaloosa coloring covering their hips, were resting before battle as they stood with one back leg cocked and their bodies warming under heavily blanketed saddles. The sorrel turned his head as Jack flipped the light switch and in a few seconds, the horse fully opened his eyes against the dim barn bulb. The sorrel displayed an Appaloosa pattern that capped his hips with snow-white hair and the bay looked like a smeary leopard with conglomerate spots resembling rattlesnake skin.

Jack loosened the lead rope of the large bay gelding and backed him from the tie stall. Even a well-trained athlete like Jack had difficulty mounting with such cumbersome clothing and only the oversized, flat-bottomed roper stirrups, that looked more like ladder steps than stirrups, made it possible for him to use his snowmobile boots. Jack was equipped for battle.

At first the cattle wouldn't move and stood like frozen Hereford statues. Jack knew it was useless to hoot and holler like a movie cowboy because the wind would carry his voice away, making it barely a whisper to the cattle. Jack sic'd Pal at cows on the edge of the herd. The biting at their heels was more painful than the driving wind and although the dog had seen better years, the cattle were no match for the shepherd's quickness. After an hour of milling in circles, the snow was reduced from feet to inches and in a small area the cattle were safe from suffocation.

As the riding shifts changed through the night, the men sustained their strength because of Danni's cooking. She boiled up a pot of stew that simmered longer than the wind blew. Every time Jack put his feet under the kitchen table, he devoured whatever Danni put in front of him and before he collapsed into his easy chair for a nap, he complimented her cooking.

Like soldiers trapped in a foxhole who stay friends for life, a voiceless dependency and respect was developing. Saving the cattle was their battle and all three people were determined that the fight would not be lost. Mother Nature is triumphant in all wars, but fighting her elements wins the battle of temporary self-preservation.

The wind stopped as quickly as it started. By noon, wet saddle blankets were pulled off the two horses and they were turned out in a corral separate from the cattle. The sorrel gelding was noticeably lame. Jack could tell by the horse's gait that the sorrel had injured his stifle, the horse equivalent of the human knee, when he slipped on an ice patch. Jack hoped to never become a bench warmer because of a knee injury.

Fatigue did not prevent the two geldings from locating an area with bare dirt, blown free of snow. Rolling over several times to scratch and massage themselves, they proved their worth. Jack's dad had explained to him as a small child that the athletic ability of a horse could be judged by the number of times a horse rolled over. With an instinctively serious tone, his dad always smiled about a horse being worth $100.00 for every roll. The sorrel was worth more than the bay.

One old cow died. Unable to keep moving, she went down in the herd and was trampled to death. The rest of the Herefords started bellering. Feeding the critters seemed a minor chore and by early afternoon, the older cows were lying down closing eyes as they chewed their cud.

Late afternoon brought sunshine, contrasting sharply with the life-stalking blizzard of only hours before. North Dakota looked surreal and imaginary. The wind had made the landscape into either snowdrifts or bare dirt. Danni's little Ford Ranger had, by chance, been parked so the wind had blown it completely snow free. Relaxing in his easy chair, Uncle John became philosophical before his first of many evening naps, "Looks like you got a thousand-acre parking lot in the middle of North Dakota."

No travel was possible. Unless some other form of transportation appeared, the pickups and their passengers would be staying until the snowplow went by and the driveway was plowed. Uncle John's Arctic Cat snowmobile was fired up and Jack asked Danni if she wanted to help him get some emergency supplies. Dressed in Uncle John's long underwear and snowmobile suit, Danni wrapped both arms around Jack's middle. Harvey, North Dakota was only ten miles from the ROCKING J. Danni thought that the distance sounded like forever away, but in less than twenty minutes they were cruising down main street.

Other mechanical snow horses charged like internal combustion steeds as their riders jousted with the drifted snow banks. Jack's father had told him about going to town after blizzards. On horseback, it was an all day project.

Jack introduced Danni to everyone. Cumbersome clothing could not hide her beauty, made even more striking by the redness on her wind-burned cheeks. They walked into the local cafe as the last remnants of Dakota sunlight dropped below the horizon. The place was chock-full of cowboys in snowmobile gear. In such weather, stocking hats were more functional than a funky looking cowboy hat. Those were saved for summer weather and dancing. There were no Rexall wranglers and Danni seemed a little surprised to not see one real cowboy. Jack simply told her that people living in Massachusetts hardly ever see a Pilgrim either. That was just one more thing she loved about Jack—his sense of humor.

The porcelain count in the restaurant was high. That referred to the crock of conversation that contained a mixture of truth and fantasy. Weather, crops and cattle, but especially horses, were the hot-stove topics. Danni was the only woman. All the guys were surprised to see their local hero, Jack, with such a fine piece of work. When they learned that she could ride a horse they were even more impressed. She tried to describe fancy English riding, called dressage, in which a mount is guided through a series of movements without perceptible cues. After she described it, she wrote the word down on a napkin. The cowboys failed their French pronunciation test and said "dress-edge."

Even though these cowboys could break and ride the toughest broncs in the West, they didn't care if a horse was on the right or left lead. Danni explained that horses put one foot ahead of the other both in front and back when they canter. One of Jack's friends, bowlegged with toes pointing inward, then needed to learn the word "canter," which to him meant "gallop."

The boys learned horsemanship from a girl in a snowmobile suit. Melding civilized and primitive upbringings had already become a fascinating lifestyle for Danni and Jack. When an anonymous smart alec plugged the jukebox, all the cowboys wished they were Jack as culture and country blended on the smallest dance floor Danni had ever seen. Through every song, fast and slow, they danced until all the quarters were gone. As sweat started to flow, layers of winter gear lay strewn beside the counter stools and more quarters were plugged until the cash register was dry of twenty-five cent change. Danni found one more quarter in Jack's front pocket and asked if they could play that one particular song.

The action stopped. All the cowboys and Danni listened as Willie sang, "Angel Flying too Close to the Ground."

On the way home Danni held closer to Jack. As the whirring machine numbed and the bobbing light hypnotized, she buried her head behind Jack's shoulder. She could feel his muscles contract and relax as he throttled and turned. Squeezing him even tighter, she made her mouth say things that she had never said before because she knew Jack couldn't hear them anyway.

Turning north for the last quarter mile, the Arctic Cat engine dropped to an idle. The stillness of the clear afterstorm sky outlined the spilling Big Dipper. The steel horse crawled up the driveway that was blanketed with snow, making it a flat continuum with the rest of North Dakota. The road seemed to extend into forever. Still facing toward the north, the engine died and they both looked at the Big Bear.

The clear subzero night was not enough to make them cold. Bodies warmed from the inside keep the cold away naturally. Danni unzipped Jack's suit to the waist and while facing him, put both arms around the frame that stood for security, strength and most of all, love. Long reciprocating arms swallowed her until she felt like another breath would not be possible. The Dipper's light marked the features of both faces and their eyes exchanged instincts from the most primitive mind. Her cold nose brushed across his warm lips. They nuzzled each other as they ambled with clasped bodies, pausing with dragging feet to refresh their feelings. Halfway to the ROCKING J ranch house, they turned as one from south to north. Their heads tilted toward the winter sky. With no preparation, but in complete unison, Jack Steele and Danni Penfield whispered, "That's the Big Dipper."

The whole world seemed right.

The steps to the house were now cleanly scooped. Uncle John had been busy. The single 75-watt light bulb above the kitchen table was still lit. Jack wondered why his uncle would be awake at midnight. Jack looked through the window and could see Uncle John's large hands clumsily scratching a note on a wide-lined piece of paper—the kind he used for writing letters. As Danni entered, Uncle John glanced at her for only an instant and then quickly diverted his eyes. "I was just writing you a note. A few minutes ago I got a phone call. It was about your dad. He had a heart attack. You're supposed to get home right away. They don't expect him to live."

The next morning Danni's pickup followed the county snowplow for the first ten miles to the state plowed roads in Harvey, North Dakota. A cloud of snow-spray blurred Jack's visage of his disappearing love. Squinting his eyes against the bright morning sun, Jack thought he could see Danni's hands clutched to the steering wheel. The little red truck, led down a single-lane snow-grooved road behind the huge diesel powered V-plow, disappeared from sight with the roar of the diesel engine hanging in the sub-zero Dakota stillness. For a few moments, the sound retained its loudness, and then, after several painful minutes of memory, the snowplow roar in Jack's ears slowly decreased to zero decibels. With his senses vacant, Jack was left with the richness of his thoughts and the memory of Danni's touch on that North Dakota winter night.

Jack stood with a frozen stance for several minutes and fixated his gaze on the ROCKING J mailbox, where Danni waved her last good-bye. He wondered if Danni would ever write to him. Jack knew that he would write to her and at the thought of sending Danni a Valentine's Day card, began to sense his own breathing and heart beat.

Jack had long ago become convinced that he controlled his own self-preservation and happiness. Now he questioned his own assumptions and wondered if he would ever see another snow cloud that hung so heavily with the memories of Jack Steele and Danni Penfield.

Jack stayed at the ranch to help Uncle John break colts.

Deep snow provided good footing for the young colts and pleasant landing in case of a wreck. The green colts were gathered into a small corral where Uncle John, with a backhand flip, rolled his lariat loop over a wild colt's head. The free colts scattered while the captured one was snubbed to a large post in the center of the corral. The smart ones soon learned to give to the pull of the rope and shortly, the saddle horn of Jack's saddle and a 1200-pound, snake-skinned Appaloosa gelding replaced the snubbing post. Jack ponied the young colts being careful not to get a front foot in the face when the colts jumped forward to escape poll pressure from their pulling halters. By riding in small inward spiraling circles, the young horses achieved mental maturity in minutes. Soon they were successfully avoiding even the slightest pull by moving straight ahead with the old pony horse.

Nostrils flared and Jack could feel the hot, sweet breath on his right arm before it crystallized into steam. Having grown thick winter hair coats, vapor clouds rose above the perspiring colts, making them smell skunky and wilder than the wild animals they had been only minutes before. With properly timed training, domestication quickly became feigned. These selectively bred Illusion progeny had been chosen to be the next set of using horses for the ROCKING J. Ranch horses had to be both tame and tough. The Cayuses that didn't train quickly were sold at the Harvey sale barn. Along with the lame or badly conformed, they would make the long trip to France wrapped in frozen rectangular paper packages.

Circling the corral, Jack sensed the fear of each colt and started talking in quiet soothing tones as he stroked their faces. Rubbing their foreheads, placing his hand gently over each eye, scratching deeply into their manes and patting alongside the neck were training actions Jack had known since childhood. He only wished that Danni could have watched, and more importantly, participated as his comrade, helpmate and woman. She had planned to stay for the entire semester break and would have been a welcome addition to the ROCKING J staff. Jack imagined Danni at the bed of her dying father.

In a Chicago hospital, Dr. Penfield was now in his patients' position. Every doctor must wonder how his end will come. Despite all modern contrivances, every physician must admit to himself that the grim reaper also waits to swing his scythe at the Achilles heel of the healer. Tubed and catheterized, he lay waiting for his only real hope of survival—Danni.

She had never seen her father so helpless and Danni was unable to control the anxiety accumulated during the 14-hour trip back to her father's bedside. Danni cried tears of regret and guilt. She was not tough enough to even think about losing the only man she loved. Of course, she loved Grandpa, and now Jack, but they were different. She had spent her whole life with her father. Her mother died when she was only hours old. Danni grew up with a mother who only lived in stories and pictures. Dr. Penfield never remarried and devoted his entire life to his daughter. Until Jack, there had been only one man in her life. Dr. George Penfield.

Danni's guilt was ripping at her insides and halfway down the long hallway to the hospital cafeteria, she made a 180 degree turn realizing that she wasn't hungry. If only she could have been at her father's side. If only she hadn't been with Jack. If only she had not told her father about Jack. If only she had stayed at home. If only she had enrolled at Northwestern like her father wanted.

Her mind was totally obsessed and her desperate desire to be with her father prematurely created a pre-marital divorce of Danni and Jack Steele. Her euphoric ranch experience of only hours before now seemed like a dim snow-clouded memory. Her feelings for Jack were confused and ambivalent. She hated herself. She was angry with Jack. He had talked her into going with him to the ROCKING J. Guilt was becoming internalized and was making Danni feel ashamed.

According to Danni's interpretation of events, her letter arrived at the Penfield residence, stating that she would be spending the next two weeks with Jack. Moments later, a 911 call was made to the hospital by a breathless voice. Her father's desperate cry for help, she thought, may have hoarsely whispered both the words "ambulance" and "Danni." How could she ever forgive herself—and Jack—for what they had done to her father? Probably Jack was too busy at the ranch and wouldn't even care.

Back at the ROCKING J, the training was progressing quickly. By the second day, the long yearlings were about to be saddled. They were still skittish and needed more desensitization. A 40-foot rope slung over Jack's shoulder would provide restraint as each young horse learned to trust. A drag rope had been attached to each colt's halter and Jack quickly grabbed the closest. This time the snubbing post didn't show the first wiggle and the safety knot hung loosely tied to the post. Each colt had learned to accept what could not be changed. The uncompromising halter no longer stretched their necks nor would their muscles strain against the thick rope.

A sideline hobble, made from the soft non-burning rope, partially immobilized each colt by pulling one hind leg off the ground. As Jack worked around the colts he remained constantly vigilant. In this game, there was no room for mistakes. One error in judgment or one wrong move put both horse and trainer at risk of injury. Jack's mental preoccupation with Danni didn't help his horse concentration.

By noon, all six colts were wearing what Uncle John called training saddles, which only meant the saddles had been in many storms. Jack went to the ranch house to make a bachelor dinner. Danni could have left the corral early and had the grub waiting. Where was Danni now that he needed her. Jack wondered if he should try to call. Or maybe Danni would call him.

After the tenth ring, Jack returned the old rotary phone to its station. What he didn't know is that Danni was huddled by her father's bedside hoping for a miracle. An angiogram, a procedure requiring a life signing away signature, was scheduled for the following morning. Dye would be inserted via a small catheter into a large leg vein that eventually led to her father's heart. X-rays taken while the opaque substance circulated throughout his heart would reveal the exact extent and location of damage. With all this on her mind and still feeling that her letter may have caused the heart attack, Danni's preoccupation with Jack and his ranch seemed a century away.

Results of the angiogram indicated that Dr. Penfield needed open heart surgery to repair coronary blockages. At least three bypasses would be used to provide collateral circulation and a large leg vein would be excised for the raw material.

Danni was worried sick. She ate only to prevent starvation and sleep came fitfully. Her active life style that had included daily exercise was filled with dismayed worry. Jack seemed less important with each passing day. Her life was on hold. If her father survived surgery, a long process of rehabilitation and aftercare would require that she transfer to Northwestern, as her father had desired from the start.

Another North Dakota blizzard hovered on the western horizon. Jack stripped his russet-colored Hereford saddle from the last colt. The saddle was Jack Steele's Christmas Eve present from Annie and James Steele. His parents died fifty-seven days later in a collision with a drunk driver. The Hereford saddle had intrinsic value. The pommel leather was bruised, scuffed and stained, but the bull hide tree made the saddle nearly unbreakable. It had broken many a colt but no colt had ever broken it.

Jack and his saddle had been victorious again and the saddle had a few more trophy marks. Jack would need some time to heal sore muscles. The yearlings would be turned out until spring when Jack and his personal saddle would refresh their memories of January training.

Jack kneeled beside the saddle on the pretense of examining the stirrup leathers. But Uncle John knew better. Before returning to college, Jack needed to say good-bye to the memories in the saddle leather.

The radio announcer was predicting another North Dakota blizzard that would strike by morning and stay until dark. If the storm persisted, Uncle John, riding solo shifts, would become too fatigued to keep the cattle moving. Some would suffocate and with the loss of too many head of cattle, the ROCKING J might also die.

Jack couldn't stay at the ranch to help Uncle John. His football scholarship required that he to return to Nebraska for interim weight-training and conditioning.

Jack boarded the Greyhound bus. Uncle John stood on the snow-covered blacktop as Jack, on the first step of the bus, turned to shake hands and say good-bye. With extra firmness, Uncle John squeezed Jack's right hand and with a solid smack of his left hand on Jack's muscular shoulder, assured Jack that the ROCKING J would survive. It always had.

DAKOTA FRAZIER STEELE

The Evanston novelty shop windows, reddened with crepe paper and heart shaped candy boxes, extracted Danni's mind from the February snowstorm that threatened the entire Great Lakes Region. She was barely aware of the large snowflakes or the biting Lake Michigan wind that made eddies inside her untied parka. Focusing on the storm within, she could care less about the superficial feeling of her skin. She stood for too long with her eyes fixed on a Valentine's display window featuring ponies and horses and unicorns and the winged Pegasus. Wind could not dry her cheeks.

Semester break seemed eons ago. Danni ached for Jack. Her unspoken acceptance of her father's edicts made her appear tough on the outside, but Danni's ego-protective shell crumbled when she was alone and dared to sense her true feelings. On the outside she seemed well adjusted. Only when her internal physiological changes broke through her defensive crust of repression and denial, did she even notice that something was radically different.

Her facial skin, usually so fresh and natural, had drawn tight against her high cheekbones giving a sunken look to her entire face. She felt no particular need to eat and when she was able to force food, her stomach gnawed with nausea as though refusing to provide sustenance for her body. In the mornings she vomited nothing.

It was as though she was having an allergic reaction to something previously unknown to her body. As in organ transplantation, the host tries to reject the foreign invader. Nothing edible seemed to agree with her. Danni's athletic frame shrunk day by day and she thought the depression of leaving Jack and the tribulation of her father's illness would soon be over and she would be restored to full strength and vigor. After more than a month she began to wonder.

Danni's doctor smiled and said, "I've got some good news for you, young lady. There's nothing wrong with you that eight more months won't cure. Your husband will probably be more happy than you to know that you have successfully conceived."

Danni smiled back and simply said, "Thank you. I'm sure he'll be glad too." She didn't want the doctor to know that she wasn't married. Danni had found and worn the ring Mary Penfield, her mother, had accepted with a shortened lifetime oath. Danni had correctly guessed that she might be carrying Jack Steele's child.

With a confused mind, Danni reviewed her choices and only the ones that included bearing Jack's child were even considered. Should she drop out of Northwestern and return to Jack? Should she stay and continue to take care of her father? Should she even call Jack and let him know about their baby? Should she tell her father?

The last question was answered first. Being a medical man and seeing the deterioration of his daughter—and the morning sickness—Dr. George Penfield had suspected that Danni was pregnant. As Danni attended to his needs, he could trace her condition. First, he too thought her mood swings were related to depression over the loss of Jack and the burden of his care. But after Danni returned from her medical appointment in a mood of confused excitement, he knew something was different.

"Danni, I think we need to talk." Dr. Penfield almost ordered. "I've noticed that you've gone from being depressed to being almost euphoric and I know that you aren't a bipolar person. What's going on?"

Hesitantly, but with reserved pride, Danni blurted out, "Daddy I'm pregnant with Jack's baby."

Dr. George Penfield sat quietly in his chair before moving his cane and rising to his feet. "Danni, I'm going to try my best to be positive about this. I know that neither you nor I would consider terminating this pregnancy. It goes against everything we both believe. But I don't want you seeing that cowboy anymore. You'll just end up with a dozen kids and live on a run-down ranch. I don't want you to have to struggle for survival like I did. I want something better for you. Since I was raised in poverty, I swore at your mother's dying breath that you and your children would have the very best."

"Anyway," continued Danni's father, "I've always wanted a man around the house and the odds are fifty-fifty that I'll have a grandson."

Danni's reaction of joyful tears required only two words, "Thanks Daddy."

Valentine's Day disappeared from the calendar without a word or card from Jack. Danni's loneliness was only compensated by the growing life within her womb. Danni wouldn't know until years later about the long letter and mushy card that Jack sent from Lincoln, Nebraska to Evanston, Illinois. It was postmarked February 12 for arrival on exactly February 14.

Dr. George Penfield heard the click of the mailbox lid and having almost nothing to occupy his time since surgery, retrieved all the mail, including Jack's correspondence.

Looking at the return address, Dr. Penfield made a decision that would change Jack and Danni's history. Angrily ripping the letter open and finding the personal Valentine's Day card inside, Danni's disapproving father decided upon the right course of action even before reading what the letter said:

Dear Danni,

I've been wondering what happened to you since you didn't show up for second semester. I hope your dad is getting better. I'll never forget the times we spent together. I love you more than anything else in the world. The blizzard at the ranch was terrible but you made it beautiful. I wish we could go back to the night before the storm when we were so close that even the Gods couldn't keep us apart. I can still see you in the ranch house kitchen making food for Uncle John and me. You seemed like my wife. Excuse me for saying that, but that's what I felt.

When you danced with me and hugged my chest as the machine took us home and zipped down my snowmobile suit and we looked at The Big Bear.......Can I please have you back?

If you can't come back to Nebraska for school at least let me know when you come to visit your grandpa. Also, I'm thinking of transferring to Northwestern. I contacted the football coach and he said the door is always open for someone like me. Let me know what you think of that idea. We could still be together and you could go to medical school later at Northwestern like you planned. I tried to call you many times, but always get no answer or a gruff voice that is probably your dad. It's too bad he has to feel the way he does about us.

I hope you like the card.

Love to you and you love me. Jack (alias The Dakota Colt)

There was not one hint of guilt as George Penfield read Jack's personal love letter to Danni. Only disgust, anger and resolve circled through his newly implanted coronary arteries nearly causing them to explode. He promised himself to do everything possible to terminate his daughter's relationship with that "no good cowboy that thought football was more important than education."

Danni endured.

As the growing months of Danni's pregancy seemed to widen her outlook, they constricted her father's perspective. Dr. Penfield's rejection of his agrarian upbringing had made him perceptually analagous to the horses he drove as he cultivated Nebraska corn. He was blind to Danni's true needs and Jack's good qualities. He was blind to the true unity of Danni and Jack. He was blind to the future of his unborn grandchild. But most of all, he was blind to his own dependency on Danni.

Like a plodding Belgian work horse wearing bridle blinders, he crashed down the corn rows not stopping to sample the sweet young stalks. Nor could he tolerate being alarmed by the world outside his narrow view. He only saw straight ahead. Dr. Penfield's promise to raise Danni "right" made her totally dependent on Daddy.

But as she matured, the relationship became symbiotic. They needed each other to survive. Blinded to Danni's needs as a woman, and Jack's strengths as a man, Dr. Penfield pursued his selfish interests. He would not alarm himself with the unknown world beyond. His psychologically imposed visual field cut made his blinders more real than the physical kind worn by the cultivating horses. At least the horses could see normally after they were relieved of their leather obstructions.

Jack's five-month intrusion had temporarily suspended Danni's dependency on her father. For a brief interim, Jack was the only man in her life. After Dr. Penfield's heart bypass surgery, Danni became a parent to her own father. Danni's pregnancy seemed to validate Dr. George Penfield's hostile feelings toward Jack.

Internal blindness snowballed into a perfectionistic obsession in which no man—even Jack—was good enough for his daughter. His heart attack, triggered by Danni's association with Jack, made him dependent upon Danni. She was his sole emotional support and provider. Danni's unborn child would be the son he had never known.

A white coat appeared in the waiting room. "Congratulations Dr. Penfield. Your daughter is doing fine and your grandson has a full head of hair. All seven pounds eight ounces seem to be healthy."

Against her father's wishes, Danni named him

"Dakota."

"Dakota Steele."

"Dakota Frazier Steele."

Little Dakota was an apple that didn't fall far from the tree. Like a selectively bred animal, he seemed to have inherited the best from both parents. His development was as hurried as his walk and his intellect as sharp as his accelerated tongue.

When he was only two, Danni bought her child an eleven-inch pony saddle that she strapped to a living room hassock. Dakota practiced cinching up other furniture and could soon ride every chair, coffee table and couch in his grandpa's house.

Danni's scrapbook, featuring only Jack Steele, the father that Dakota had never known, was by now lined with hundreds of newspaper clippings and pictures from the *Lincoln Star Journal*. On the cover was a large picture of Jack that Danni had taken on her only visit to the ROCKING J. That was a real Dakota Memory. Little Dakota was the living proof.

Favorite bedtime stories of Dakota's were always the ones that featured Jack, football and the ROCKING J. "Tell me the scary horse story again. The one about Curly." Dakota, begging like a typical four year-old, demanded that the story be told over and over again.

"Well, a long time ago," began Danni, "There was a man who lived on a ranch way out west. It is so far away that the clock has to go around twice before we could get to his place. He lived in Colorado and raised red cows that have white faces. The man's name was Joe Steele. Your name is Dakota Steele. He was your great-grandfather. He rode horses almost everyday. His favorite horse was named Curly because he had white hair that looked like he had a permanent. One day, Curly got caught in barbed wire and was bleeding really bad. So when Curly died, your great-grandpa, who was called Joe Steele, took all the hair off his favorite horse. They call that skinning because the skin and hair come off together."

"But Mommy, you forgot the part where Great-Grandpa shot Curly right between the eyes," corrected Dakota.

"That's right, he shot Curly to put him out of his misery. When Joe skinned out Curly, he even left his head on and then shipped his hide to Minnesota to get preserved. That means so he could become a rug on the floor. Curly isn't just a story. He's real. I saw him at your daddy's ranch in North Dakota. Great-Grandpa Joe gave him to Grandpa Jim and now your dad, Jack, has him. Curly is dead but in a way he's still alive. He's right in the middle of the ROCKING J living room floor. He's got scary eyes made of glass and his ears are pointy just like a real horse." Danni clarified.

"Mom, can we see Curly some time?" Dakota was ready. "Will he be my horse some time? I want to ride him like Great-Grandpa did."

Danni's eyes moistened as she told Dakota, "I guess he's kind of your horse already. I'm sure that Jack Steele would want you to ride Curly. He'd love to see a little Dakota Colt like you. We can't go there because it takes too long and your dad hasn't seen me in a really long time and would be too surprised if we just drove in."

"I like surprises. Couldn't we just go there to see Curly? Mom, what about that weird horse? The one with all the black spots. Tell me that story. That one's more funner than Curly even." Dakota insisted that Danni retell the mysterious Illusion story.

"Kota, Mom doesn't know much about the weird horse. His name was Illusion. He was your grandpa's stud. That means a daddy horse. He had lots of babies and lots of them looked like him. He was all spotty kinda like a leopard. Your daddy wouldn't tell me any more. He said that the story of Illusion was a family secret. Only your daddy and his uncle know the whole story." Danni was interrupted.

"Mom, aren't we part of The Dakota Colt's family?" Kids like Dakota always asked the hardest questions.

Spurs dug into the wooden horse's sides as rockers galloped over the carpeted floor. The small hand grabbed the white mop string mane as the other hand held fast to the dowel that passed through a hole drilled in the horse's head. The fake horse loved the rocking that flipped his string mane and ducked his head with each rocking revolution. Danni busied herself in the kitchen making soothing noises that mothers send to their children when contented. Dakota jumped off his rocking horse, "Thanks Mommy. I love that horse. What's his name?"

"The man didn't tell me his name. He's your first horse. You get to choose his name." Danni reached down swooping up Dakota in her arms and swung him back and forth through the air and then, spinning all the way around, lounged toward the living room couch where the pair collapsed in a pile of happy screams and laughter.

"Can I just name him 'Horse'?" Dakota sounded so much like his father already. Danni remembered how Jack had said every cowboy calls his horse, "Horse" and his dog, "Dog" and his woman, "yes Ma'am."

"That's the greatest name I ever heard." Danni was not only trying to be a loving and accepting mother, but actually wanted Dakota's new rocking horse to be named in honor of Jack's humorous, but meaningful, expression.

Dakota squealed like a shoat being held by a back leg as he kicked free from his mother's half-clasped hand and made a dive for the horse's rocker legs. The Pinocchio of rocking horses dropped to his side like a trick horse trained to play dead on command. "Look Mom, 'Horse' is sleeping. He must be tired. I better give him some food when he gets up."

"Horses eat oats and hay. That's their food." Danni believed that Jack would approve her expansion of Dakota's horse language and she planned on giving her son as much information about Jack and his ranch as could be done vicariously. He needed to know about his father. Someday Little Dakota and Big Dakota would meet face-to-face and like the colts she remembered from Jack's ranch, would play in the blizzard snow while she cooked lefse on the cast iron cookstove. With glazed eyes, Danni imagined the steaming tea kettle and curled burnt orange peels that blended with ranch smells creating a potpourri fit for the finest perfume.

Moving to Rochester, Minnesota, Dakota's mother suddenly became a famous doctor. When he talked to other kids, his mom's doctoring and his dad's ranching suited his enlarged six year-old vocabulary. Yet, when Danni picked him up at school she just looked like Mom. Dakota's first grade teacher,

Rocking horse, named "Horse" by Dakota Frazier Steele

Ms. Chadwell, brightened Danni's day when school was dismissed for parent-teacher conferences. "Dakota is a gifted young man. I use those words because he doesn't act like a kid. He's way ahead of his age in every aspect of development."

On the playground, even a casual observer could see that the little Dakota Colt's gazelle-like moves were something unique and special. Mr. Ryan Olson, a sixth grade teacher, was also a YMCA coach for the youngest Minnesota Vikings. Seeing Danni and Dakota leave school one day, he introduced himself and asked Danni about enrolling her son in YMCA football. Winking at Dakota, Mr. Olson bragged on his newest little league superstar, "This young man runs faster than the football can be thrown and when it hits his hands the ball sticks every time."

"Please Mom, let me play football. I'm really fast. And I know The Dakota Colt would want me to play. You told me I look just like him." Dakota had decided to play football. His mother wisely agreed.

"You said something about The Dakota Colt. How would you know about him? He was the greatest wide receiver in college football until he got hurt. But you're way too young to remember him." The coach wanted to know more.

"He's my dad." Dakota explained his Crazy Legs Hirsch running style.

Danni's eyelids squinted to a slit against the September sun. She could see the churning legs of her son that brought her daily to the practice field. Even on days when practice wasn't formally scheduled, Dakota enlisted his mother's quarterback arm.

Danni's autumn-watching eyes turned inward where the setting sun elicited an imprinted Cornhusker memory. Seven barren years and two vacant months, time enough for the loss of most memory, had only brightened the dimly lit hallways that stored Danni's secret thoughts of Jack. Jack Steele.

Danni recalled how The Dakota Colt, who started the fall as a red shirt freshman, had taken the country with his galloping stride and circus catches. She recalled how she had arranged for a meeting between her father and Jack. Dr. Penfield had watched Jack romp over the turf, snatching passes and scoring touchdowns. Nebraska won. Jack was great. She had hoped for her father's approval. She recalled with regret that Jack's All-American performance was still not enough to satisfy her father.

During the flag football season, the Little Dakota Colt bucked and kicked his way all over the turf. Mr. Olson's coaching included a reverse play in which the wide receiver became a running back. Dakota played tackle football with his older neighborhood friends. But at the YMCA games, everyone played flag football. Like a free-galloping yearling, flapping fabric evaded grabbing hands as his darting legs rambled toward the goalposts.

Mr. Olson's voice awakened Danni from a Sunday afternoon nap. "I'm putting together some names of kids for the punt, pass and kick contest. Can I put Dakota's name on the list? I think he can win his age division."

At Dakota's next game, Mr. Olson's attention was distracted from football. He called the end-around reversal for enough touchdowns to win the game and one mother became a twenty-something cheerleader as her son scored four touchdowns. Ryan Olson was watching Dakota's mother. He was wondering if Danni would like his company or if she only liked his coaching.

Mr. Olson had noticed that Danni signed her name on the PPK entry as Danni Penfield and that Dakota's last name was Steele. Little Dakota let the cat out of the bag when he told Mr. Olson all about Curly and Illusion and how they lived on his dad's ranch in North Dakota. He also told about the scrapbook that featured his dad—made by his mom.

Danni started the engine of the new red Bronco and leaving the parking lot, Dakota waved a whole-arm goodbye to his coach. "You really like Mr. Olson don't you?" Danni had both noticed and felt the attraction.

Dr. George Penfield didn't live long enough to see his grandson win the regional PPK contest. And Jack, watching the half-time show being broadcasted from Soldier's Field in Chicago, didn't realize that the young kid with his same last name and the first name of his home state was his own growing seed. Ryan Olson followed Dakota's throwing arm and kicking leg to the finals.

"Hey Mr. Olson, can we stop at the Dairy Queen on"...............Dakota was interrupted by his mother who was allowing Ryan Olson to drive her Bronco.

Chocolate smears joined ketchup splotches as Dakota inhaled a hot fudge sundae and three hot dogs. Ryan and Danni sipped on diet cokes. "He must have a hollow leg where he puts all that food. You know, during the football season I think he's grown two inches and gained ten pounds of solid muscle." Mr. Olson knew how to make Danni proud and her son happy.

Dakota had become a vehicle for Ryan Olson's affections toward Danni. She was suspicious of developing a relationship with the coach who was rebounding from a short marriage and a long divorce. The coach knew that Danni could never really love anyone like she had loved Jack. The proof was in her scrapbook.

Kicking his leg higher than his head, Dakota's right arm came with strong momentum and full over-hand motion. The baseball rocketed to a blazing little league speed of 58 miles per hour. Dakota's fist smacked certainty into the pocket of his glove as he snagged the catcher's errant return. In one synchronized leaping motion, his legs split, scissored and set squarely with the pitcher's mound before dropping exactly on the rubber.

"What a catch!" Mr. Olson recognized Dakota's unique ability.

"The way he's eating me out of house and home he better be developing or I'm really wasting a lot of food." Danni nudged the man sitting next to her who had become her closest confidant and Dakota's surrogate father.

Through football, basketball and baseball, Ryan Olson and Danni Penfield had watched Dakota's six and seven year-old performances. Even though his fastball breezed by the bats of older kids and his jump shot was already one-handed, Dakota's game was football. Gliding with air beneath feet that barely seemed to touch ground, his hands glued almost tightly enough to extract the VOIT lettering from the mite-sized pigskin.

School always began after Labor Day. Because his birthday was in October, Dakota would be an extra-large second grader.

A light snow covered the wide white lines of the football field as the huddled four footers gathered around Mr. Olson. "Dakota take the ball and run wide around left end."

Danni's red Bronco zipped into a parking spot just in time. Number 80, with legs slashing the crusty snow, broke into the open like a galloping and unrestrained colt turned loose for his first romp after weaning. Breaking into a jog before reaching the sidelines, Danni raised her arms overhead like a referee signaling a touchdown. Then she shoved her right fist into the air as her body twisted toward the turf. Danni could barely inhibit the blood-curdling scream that begged to release itself.

"Settle down Mom." Mr. Olson calmly advised. "We don't get that excited anymore when Dakota makes one of his patented long runs. We just kind of expect him to run like that. Stick around 'cause after the game we're going for pizza. I've got a surprise for the kids."

Pepperoni and sausage churned with post-game sweat and turf stains created a masculine fragrance at two tables of little league Vikings. Purple and white pom-pons wiggled in unison with each head bob and jaw crunch. The stocking hats, purchased by Mr. Olson as season ending presents, stayed tight to the skulls. Not even one hand reached to jerk the prized gift from another head and the only disturbances to the hats were the proud new owners' pizza covered fingers that occasionally reached upward to ensure that the label "Minnesota Vikings" was still attached.

"I think they're having fun," Mr. Olson spoke with hyperbole.

"I guess so!" Danni reinforced his too obvious statement. "It's really nice that you bought those stocking hats. I know Dakota will go to bed with his. He'll wear it until it can walk by itself. But that's AOK. I don't have much time for laundry these days. Tomorrow I have to go to Red Wing to see a new patient. I guess a crazy horse dragged him by the leg. It sounds like a pretty gruesome wreck. Those horse accidents still frighten me. I can really relate to those patients. I know about horses and had a horse accident with a minor brain trauma myself. Anyway, thanks for the stocking hat and thanks for helping Dakota so much in football."

YEARS

As the years passed, miscommunication and misunderstanding formed pacts of ignorance. Jack and Danni came separately and independently to the conclusion that, although they wanted to be together, the circumstances would never permit their union. Dr. George Penfield, Danni's father, had been influential. Through guilt or obligation, Danni decided to stay with Dad. To Danni, that automatically meant rejection of Jack.

Deciding not to waste his time with someone so preoccupied, Jack registered for more semesters of Nebraska education and trekked to the ROCKING J on a Danniless Greyhound Bus. Uncle John was always glad to see Jack and often asked about Danni. "Where's that gal that helped us survive the storm?"

Gazing longingly out the ranch house window where Danni's little truck had been parked, Jack's voice faltered. "I just never hear from her............since she went back to be with her dad............guess it's over between us............was the best time of my life.........when we were together.........blizzard was tops.........guess she just doesn't want to see me anymore."

In Evanston, Illinois the phone rang off the hook. There was no answer because Danni was attending to her hospitalized father. Her priorities had changed. While she still loved Jack and thought constantly about him, her loyalty to her father was greater than her love for Jack.

As Danni dressed her father's leg wound he mumbled something about contacting Jack. Her strong hands had given way to sleepless fatigue and resentment in her insides consumed the few calories she cared to eat. The vein transplanted from George Penfield's leg was doing well in his heart. Stripped from his left leg, the vein no longer supplied the needed blood to his fading extremity. Dr. Penfield's infected leg was becoming swollen and purple-colored.

Diverting her gaze, Danni fumbled with submissive and slowly formed words, "I never hear from Jack anymore. I think you were right. He wasn't the man for me. I guess I just fell for him because of who he was and I didn't think enough about our future together. Besides, Northwestern is a better school and I can be with you." Danni's father had finally won the battle against Jack. Dr. Penfield was in full control of his daughter's life.

Becoming a grandfather seemed to have softened Dr. Penfield's austere personality. Little Dakota was his favorite fishing buddy. While Danni attended classes and studied at the library, Grandpa and Dakota tended the house. On holidays, Little Dakota traveled to Nebraska much like his mother had when she was a small girl. His indulgent great-grandparents waited for the sound of his quick little steps.

Jack and Danni's early years of separation dropped into the chasm of time and the calendar pages turned one month upon another. Jack amazed everyone but himself as his bulging hamstrings shot his body from Earth to Ozone. Jumping like a human projectile, his out-stretched hands smacked the pigskin to his chest. Time after time he returned safely to Earth like a lucky astronaut with nine cat-lives in his knees.

Then, one day, two linebackers made a sandwich of a Big Red knee. One bone crunch removed the name "Jack

Steele" from the NFL scouts list and the nickname "Dakota Colt" became a condolence in sports headlines that Danni searched daily.

The Lincoln, Nebraska newspaper, which carried details of the Dakota Colt's receptions, yards and touchdowns, arrived secretly in Danni's rented post office box. Danni kept her strangle hold on the distant memory of Jack and the recent black and white interviews and pictures in *The Lincoln Journal Star* seemed to tighten her grasp. When she looked at her Dakota Colt Scrapbook, there was a small child who wondered why his mommy looked at that book so much. When he was old enough to understand that books could tell stories, Dakota asked his mommy to tell about the man in the pictures.

Danni never told little Dakota anything bad about his father.

Miles of distance separated Jack and Danni. In a blizzard-filled time capsule their thoughts lived together. Neither condensed time nor infinite distance could erase their Dakota memory.

By the time Jack was a senior at Nebraska, Danni was enrolled in the Northwestern Medical School. Special high level honor program students, who had also attended Northwestern as undergraduates, could enter Medical School a year early. Danni was in that select group. Her father, with an amputated left leg caused by poor circulation following surgery, was now even more convinced that Danni belonged at Northwestern University. Danni still looked for newspaper clippings from Lincoln, Nebraska.

That autumn, during Jack's senior year at Nebraska, one of her girlfriends brought Danni an article from *USA Today*.

She turned the sports page toward Danni's face. "Isn't this the guy you used to know in Nebraska?" Danni's tears blotted the words beneath the picture of a Nebraska player, clutching his bent left knee. His Nebraska jersey displayed a wide receiver number. She didn't need to read the sportswriter's description because she knew number 80. It belonged to The Dakota Colt.

The newspaper publicity ride was over, except for a few residual articles that reviewed the Colt's exploits and consoled the readers' thirst for mayhem. Danni still didn't cancel her subscription—just in case.

Even though Danni and Jack existed apart, they lived together in a deepening Dakota memory.

As Jack returned to his Harvey, North Dakota ranch with no hope of ever pursuing his professional football dream, Danni's ambition to become a doctor was becoming reality. Northwestern University had one of the finest medical schools in the country although there were twenty-three separate departments to chose from, she still selected her childhood fantasy—Physical Medicine and Rehabilitation.

Danni's scrapbook hadn't captured any recent entries from Lincoln, Nebraska and little Dakota was starting to realize that the cowboy-football player in the pictures wasn't just some guy. He was Dad. To further educate her son, Danni rationalized that she would have to subscribe to another newspaper. She guessed that Jack had returned to his ranch and called the Harvey, North Dakota Chamber of Commerce to check on the accuracy of her hunch.

Katie, a Harvey resident with a diplomatic attitude and a pleasant sounding telephone voice, told Danni about the local newspaper. Katie also knew about Jack Steele and the ROCKING J. Danni pretended not to listen with too much interest and asked other questions about Jack's hometown. She discovered that Harvey was a railroad town. Katie mentioned that the Sheyenne river, running through town, was spelled with a "S" rather than a "C". About 3000 people lived within the city limits and there were ranches like the ROCKING J in every direction.

Danni smiled to herself as Katie described Harvey, North Dakota. It sounded like a northern version of Grandpa's North Platte, Nebraska stories.

When the Newspapers arrived, Danni told stories to her child about North Dakota in the same way that Grandpa had told tales of Nebraska. <u>Her</u> child was a Dakota memory. Maybe some day—after George Penfield died—she would call Jack to talk about <u>their</u> child.

Accumulating years, passing through distant miles, only strengthened their fantasies. Flaming memories, created on a cold Dakota night in the protected lair of the ROCKING J upstairs bedroom, burned deeper and deeper traces in Jack's soul and Danni's heart.

In her sixth year of college and her third year of medical school, Danni's residency came up with a positive match for The Mayo Clinic in Rochester, Minnesota. She crammed all the knowledge and experience she possibly could into the months from her acceptance in March until June admission. She became obsessed with her work as a Doctor of Physical Medicine and Rehabilitation. If only Jack could see her work. Jack Steele.

Danni hardly had time to ride her horse so she traded a cashier's check for the fully schooled dressage horse that

Jack had watched her ride some five years, four months and three days earlier. Maybe that was an omen, "5-4-3," a countdown to zero that would allow her to entirely forget about Jack. Still, there was a small child that would not let her forget. Dakota needed a pony and a father.

An eternity of memories drifted like Dakota snows through the sleeping and waking hours of Jack and Danni.

Jack's Philosophy major was of little value, especially in North Dakota, and his employment alternatives diminished further as Uncle John became unable to take care of himself. At first Jack tried to nurse and baby-sit his forgetful uncle. It was his experience with Uncle John that made him fully realize the anguish that Danni must have felt as her pickup followed the snowplow to the main highway. Her decision to stay with her father was much like his situation with Uncle John. He was bound to his North Dakota ranch in much the same way Danni had been bound to Chicago.

What Jack didn't know is that Danni had moved to Rochester, Minnesota.

In Rochester, Danni pushed a wheelchair slowly down the hospital corridors. A weather bulletin scanned along the bottom of the TV screen like a long piece of worded tape. A blizzard warning was being issued for the entire Upper Midwest. The storm was already in the Dakotas.

Autumn leaves hurried before the wind and the first snow curled into drifts. Danni visualized the leopard skinned Appaloosa horsehide that hung in Jack's porch and she recalled her startled reaction to the horse rug on his living room floor. She now realized how easy it would be to accept both Illusion and Curly into the ROCKING J household.

Danni's Dakota memory was now aligned with Jack's. There was no forgetting the semester-break blizzard that had set their minds on a course that ended only with Jack and Danni unity.

Danni received an emergency call and this time she didn't need to hurry home. There was no need. This time she couldn't secretly blame Jack. Her father's casket, shrouded with obligatory grief, had loosened her choking tether.

The conflict had finally ended. Danni wondered if the separation her father felt as his grandchild left for Rochester, Minnesota had dealt the final blow to his ailing heart. Bitterness was on the dying breath of Dr. George Penfield.

Danni watched her father's casket being lowered into its grave. From the deepest and most pleasure-filled corners of her mind, a veil of forbidden gratification lifted, revealing the man she could never forget. Jack. Jack Steele.

After her father's death, Danni felt the freedom to contact Jack, but in her mind she was convinced that he was involved with someone else. She had noticed that before his senior year at Nebraska, the newspapers carried a picture of The Dakota Colt with a Barbie Doll looking rodeo queen.

Danni thought the Barbie was prettier than she was. At that time, she hadn't seen Jack for two years, seven months, and nineteen days. Danni wanted to twist Jack's right hand from around the girl and peel the two lecherous arms from around his chest—the same chest that Danni had buried her face against in Jack's dorm room and the very same chest exposed by zipping down his snowmobile suit and the very same chest she had hugged with both arms. Danni also noticed the large diamond ring on the Barbie's left hand.

Kicking her intellect back into gear, Danni suppressed the stupid, jealous thoughts she had allowed herself. Besides, Jack was just another man. She could have her choice. Why settle for some Dakota cowboy?

To further discourage herself, if that was necessary, Danni became convinced that little Dakota and her profession were enough. She didn't need a man now—or maybe ever again.

What Danni didn't know is that Jack's involvement with the Barbie was superficial. Striking beauty had captured Jack, but like the loose horse he was, the Barbie could not corral him for too long. Plastic appearances were only momentary entertainment for his philosophical mind and this new girl's made-up face could never substitute for the natural loveliness of Danni.

Jack tried unsuccessfully to contact Danni and maybe, he thought, it was their fate to never be together. When Danni left Nebraska Jack had even considered transferring to Northwestern. The football coach at Northwestern was glad to hear that, but the coach at Nebraska scowled, "Don't you go ruining your life over some woman that wants to be with her father worse than you."

Jack agreed. Had he been able to see the future, he could have saved his knee and gained his heart.

Like the distant rains of summer in a Dakota drought, Jack and Danni clung to the runoff from the snows of their blizzard memories.

Occasionally, Danni would fantasize about what their life might have been like on the ranch. She could imagine herself as a small town doctor and Jack, a retired football hero, coaching the young kids. With the buildings restored and a new ranch house constructed, their own children would ride the school bus and a spotted chestnut pony. Streams of unfulfilled dreams elbowed their way into her waking thoughts like the Big Red throng. Danni's memory had preserved every Nebraska football game on a mental scroll with the post-game jostling and celebration second only in importance to Jack's healthy reappearance.

Would his name fit? Would "Danni Penfield" sound right if it was "Danni Steele" or "Dr. Danni Steele" or "Dr. Danni Penfield-Steele?" She remembered the first time she had tried his name on. Before bringing Jack his gloves, which she had forgotten anyway, she had decided the name would be Danni Steele—without the hyphen. Once, after their separation, she thought wildly of changing her name even if they weren't together, simply because she liked the sound of "Steele."

Jack dreamed too. The Barbie's temporary stay lasted until his permanent injury took away the headlines. Then another hero took his place. Danni would never have done that. Jack knew she would take care of him like she had taken care of her father. He wondered what had happened to her father. Most of all he wondered what had happened to Danni. Danni Penfield.

With his knee hurting and the night beyond late, Jack would lie awake and think of Danni sleeping beside him. He could see her contented face lost in peaceful dreams that only a newborn's wimper could intercept. Jack visualized lifting an eight-pound ten-ounce James George Steele from the cradle that had known three generations of "Steeles," and then, carrying him to the nurturing breast of the woman he loved.

Cradle at the ROCKING J, the first bed for three generations of Steele children

Sometimes, after a hard day of ranch work, The Big Dipper would rotate and spill all the water from the cup before the swelling inside Jack's left knee would be calmed by ice and aspirin. But there was no treatment for the aching in his heart. On the stars' darkest nights, when Jack was Danni blue, he'd sometimes only sleep a wink or two. And when the Moon was total new, the Dipper often spilled itself to make the morning dew.

Poetic words that Danni never heard before, were in Jack's memory now, and evermore.

The ringing phone startled Danni and brought her out of the concentration trance she often achieved while studying. The motor pathways controlling human movement transferred from an intellectual activity to a physical act as her body uncurled from the large chair and snapped to an erect stance bringing her to the phone before the third ring. In her advanced study of human functioning it was necessary to know, understand and be able to apply all the anatomy and physiology she had learned in medical school. Upon the completion of her residency, which would be only eighteen short months, Danni planned to work exclusively in a rehab setting with patients suffering traumatic brain injury.

Grabbing the phone before her six year-old son could reach the receiver, Danni's enthusiastic step was shortened as she returned to her chair to spend more time than she wanted talking to another Mayo Clinic resident who had been calling too frequently. Charles Penwick had become a nuisance. His attention to her intellectual side had extended physically and his persistent attention, while flattering, was on most occasions only an inferior substitute for another real man she had also known intimately. Jack Steele would remain forever in her mind's secret corners.

Charles was the type of man Danni's father would have been proud to call his son-in-law since he was educated, pedantic and in fact, everything that Dr. George Penfield had aspired to become as he left his father's North Platte, Nebraska ranch. Charles was raised like a gentleman. His good mannered gestures of opening doors and saying the right thing had initially entrapped Danni, probably because of the loss she felt after her father's death, but more likely because she yearned for male companionship.

After Danni hung up the receiver, she wished for a ride in Jack's ranch-beater pickup. She was beginning to hate Charles and his Mercedes. Danni would, without hesitation, trade one minute with Jack for a lifetime with Charles.

As if her frustration with the constant Jack-Charles comparison was not enough, Danni had discovered that Charles had a dark personality spot. He liked alcohol too much and sometimes, after the evening was spent, would drunkenly collapse in Danni's apartment, awakening the next morning to beg Danni's forgiveness.

Danni knew there was no way that Charles could ever measure up to the man that had made life within her body. She had been very careful to keep little Dakota's relationship with Charles superficial. Dakota, she thought, was the kind of kid that would become a man's man, like his father, and his father's father before him.

Little Dakota could pass, punt and kick a football beyond his years and Ryan Olson, Dakota's little league football coach, had persuaded Danni to let Dakota Frazier Steele's name be entered for the Rochester area PPK contest. Danni and Ryan kicked the turf as they talked. They pretended there was no magnetism.

In some ways, the recently divorced football coach reminded Danni of Jack and the contrast between Charles and Ryan seemed only to make her need for Jack more urgent. Sometimes Danni couldn't understand why she couldn't have Jack. Danni wanted Jack. One day, while on a solo walk, she made a heart shape in the sand and wrote inside: *"To Jack, All my love, danni "*

She wanted to snatch Little Dakota by his football jersey, throw him in her Bronco, a yuppie version of a pickup, and head for North Dakota. Other times, Danni wished she could just return to her grandparents in Nebraska.

Dakota was becoming a young man. Almost eight years had passed since the miracle of his conception. Secret memories were locked inside Danni's heart. They cried to be released into the arms of the man who had made her spring with life. Jack didn't know that his imaginary child had become a named and rapidly growing reality.

Little Dakota tried to make his mother feel better, but childish consolation only deepened her sorrow. She told Dakota that she was grieving and tried to explain that nothing would make Mommy feel better until the funeral was over. If only her grandfather hadn't tried to step over the power take-off and why would he do such a stupid thing while the old B-John Deere was running? Poor Grandpa Penfield. His eighty-four year-old handsome-physique, so spry and athletic, preserved beyond his own son's demise, was mangled by the revolving steel of a shieldless shaft. Danni shivered as she imagined the torturous death her grandfather, bought at the price of ultimate carelessness.

The rain-drenched streets of Crete, Nebraska were brightly lit as four blocks of slow moving headlights made a caravan behind a flashing police car. Danni was driving the first car behind the hearse. Grandma Pearl and Little Dakota rode silently. Grandma wiped intermittent tears as freezing drizzle sloshed from the windshield wipers. When the graveyard came in sight, Danni realized that Dakota had only witnessed one funeral—her father's.

He was full of eyes and questions. "How come all those guys have guns?"

Seven rifles simultaneously fired the first third of a 21-gun salute. Dakota jerked to attention as the chilling cracks of World War II weapons broke the November silence. By the third set of seven, Dakota had already learned to place his saluting hand over his right eye like the retired soldiers that were not encumbered by flags or rifles.

The First Lutheran Church basement smelled of coffee and ham sandwiches. Danni's grandmother hugged everyone. Dakota played with the other children. Danni wondered. Grandpa's death had made her think about the shortness of life. The Lutheran minister's sermon, spoken with gentle intensity, spun through her brain. "You never know when your time is up. Make this day the first day of the time you have left. Life is too short to waste."

Grandpa reminded her so much of Jack.

The synapses that she studied in medical school snapped their way throughout her entire brain, but she knew the intellectual thoughts of her forebrain would soon be consumed by primitive desires that stormed just above the brainstem. Reasoning changes emotion only with time and practice and she hadn't had enough of either to forget her grandpa. Now Jack was rising to the surface as Grandpa's living reenactment.

Leaving Dakota to his great-grandmother's care, Danni left for the short drive to Lincoln, Nebraska. For eight years her memory had been intangibly filled, like a Hollywood village, with fake doors and no occupants. She needed to find Jack and dispose of Charles.

Seeing all the Danni-Jack campus haunts she stopped at the first phone booth. "Charles, this is Danni. I have to tell you something. I think we should just be friends and professional colleagues." She clicked the receiver before Charles could reply. A few minutes later, Danni walked into the Nebraska Alumni Office.

Even the receptionist remembered Jack. "Oh. You mean The Dakota Colt. Let's see....His current address is Harvey, North Dakota. Phone number 701-....." her voice disappeared as Danni turned the computer monitor so she could read all the vital information for herself. What she really wanted to know was listed in a small box labeled martial status.

It said, **"SINGLE."** Then she asked another question. "When were these files last updated?"

"We just completed that last week," replied the gum-snapping frizzy-haired receptionist.

Danni spun toward the exit sign with her "Thank you" inaudibly swallowed by the speed of her gait. She hustled for the nearest phone.

Eight rings later, Danni heard an ear stinging voice. The receiver seemed too warm to hold against her singed ears. There was no strength in her knees. Internal aching for the feel of Jack's body became jealous fever that flashed hotly through her body's core. "Hello, this is The ROCKING J. Jack isn't here right now. But we'll be glad to call you back when we get home." The voice on the machine was female.

Danni's initial weakness almost made her drop the phone. A strong cup of coffee later, she returned to the phone and called again. 70l...... This time she concluded that the voice was a pre-recorded, standard message or the high-pitched voice was only Jack's friend. She had no reason to make this conclusion, but did so anyway. Danni left her Rochester, Minnesota phone number on the answering machine.

After hanging up, Danni realized that Jack might call before she got back from Nebraska. But after this many years, he probably didn't care anyway. She hoped that Charles Penwick's key hadn't opened the lock of her apartment door. Now she couldn't understand why she had ever been involved with that pompous nerd and really wished she hadn't given him her second key.

Stomping the mud off his boots Jack pulled one and then the other off his swollen feet. His face twisted as the grip of his hand snatched one last time to remove the left boot. With no cartilage remaining between two bones of his left knee, the joint made a grinding sound like an arthritic orchestra. Jack lowered his leg and leaned forward with both hands on both thighs. Aspirin always made his shot knee feel better.

Uncle John's chest was rising and falling with a sleep falsely deepened through medication. Irene, the county nurse, had made her daily visit to care for Uncle John. Jack read the note on the table: **"Please call me when you get home. We can go to a movie or something if you have time and aren't too tired.   Irene"**

Walking by the phone, Jack noticed that the **MESSAGE** light was flickering. Before calling Irene to ask about the quality of the movie, Jack listened to the first message he'd gotten in a week.

Irene would have to wait. Dialing quickly and with fingers trembling with more than the day's fatigue, Jack listened for an answer. After ten unanswered rings, Jack was about to conclude that the one woman he had waited to hear from for all these years, had again stood him up.

Breaking the eleventh ring in half, a slurred voice, not low enough to be that of a real man but too high to be that of a woman, answered the phone. Jack didn't bother to ask for Danni, but immediately returned the phone to its hook and called Irene. Any movie would be all right.

The movie wasn't that great and Jack, with renewed hope of talking to Danni, had been very inattentive to the county nurse. Jack drove the ten miles to the ROCKING J without Irene in his pickup. Danni was on his mind.

Once again the slurred voice punctured Jack's eardrum.

After a night of tossing and turning, that for a change was not due to an aching knee, Jack arose at 5:05 A.M. He knew Danni was an early riser and even though he suspected the worst about the voice he had heard twice already, Jack felt that he should at least have the courtesy to return Danni's call. Before morning chores, Jack tried to return Danni's call one more time. After the fourth ring, Jack heard Danni's voice. It said, "Thank you for calling. This is Dr. Danni Penfield. I'll call you back as soon as possible."

"Dr. Penfield?" Jack questioned himself, "I guess her dad finally won. Now she's just like him." The porch door slammed shut as Jack tackled another few hours of daylight. Winter would soon create dormancy across the Northern Great Plains. Jack hoped that his short message on Danni's answering machine would result in a returned phone call. If nothing else, Irene would be more interested if she answered the phone to the voice of a female. Jack whispered knowingly to himself, "That might just happen on her daily nursing visits to see Uncle John." He didn't care.

The miles back to Rochester were lengthened by the tragic death of her grandfather, but shortened by the anticipation of possibly talking to Jack. Danni hoped that Charles had gotten the message——that she was through with him—and would conveniently have disappeared from her life. All he needed to leave behind was her extra apartment key and no forwarding address.

Happy to be home, Dakota charged up the stairs of their second floor apartment and yelled back to his mother, "Hey Mom, you don't need the key. The door's already open."

Slumped over the kitchen table, with Jack Daniels emptied too recently into his throat, was the unconscious figure of Charles. Wanting to shield her son, Danni shuffled Dakota to his room where she told his favorite bedtime story—the one about The Dakota Colt. It was also her favorite story.

Then it was time to remove one alcoholic from her life forever. Jack, as a distant, but ready, memory was better than the physical presence of Charles.

With Charles heading down the road, Danni checked for phone messages not realizing that Charles' drunken stupor was brought on by her rejection and three long distance calls from area code 701—North Dakota. Charles had answered the first two and deleted the third.

In the days that followed, both Jack and Danni couldn't understand why the other person didn't try to call. Adding to Danni's confusion, was her grandmother's discovery of a large box of family valuables that had been stored in Nebraska after the Penfield residence in Evanston, Illinois had been sold. Danni began rummaging through the personal items that had belonged to her father.

Buried in the bottom of her father's valuables was a censored secret. The anger inside Danni grew as she read Jack's letter. If her father had been alive she would have made certain that his heart would have failed. Though written more than eight years earlier, the lines read as currently as *Today's Paper*. The letter insisted upon, and almost demanded, their togetherness. The letter couldn't understand what happened to Danni. The letter said The Dakota Colt would transfer to Northwestern. Worst of all, the writer of the letter had no idea that Danni was pregnant with his child.

Procrastinating about her relationship with Jack had become a way of life, but she needed to talk to someone about her dilemma. Having just seen her grandmother's strength at Grandpa's funeral, she could think of no better counselor. She needed to consider her son too. Dakota was starting to ask more and more questions about his father. He had noticed that most other kids had fathers who picked them up from school and came to watch them play football. The only father he knew was the one in his mother's scrapbook. Over the years, he had gotten to know the football hero his mother sometimes cried about when she told stories of The Dakota Colt.

Grandma helped by listening. Except for a large phone bill, Danni seemed to have arrived at a temporary solution. She would simply continue as she had been, minus the negative influences of Charles, and allow Dakota to make his own decisions when he was at an accountable age. Hearing about Dakota's football coach, Grandma's wise words helped calm the storm inside Danni that grew larger and larger like blizzard wind blowing through the ROCKING J on that Dakota night. Eighty years of wisdom suggested, with appropriate ambiguity, that a third quarter substitution might just work. Danni was left to her own interpretation and action.

Ryan Olson soon realized that he was being used as a substitute for Dakota's idol and biological father. But the coach was soon persuaded. He submitted to Danni's charismatic personality and Dakota's genetic football ability by granting Danni's wish of becoming a temporary father figure without becoming personally involved with his mother. Ryan and Dakota became big and little brothers to each other.

For one last time Danni thanked Ryan Olson. This time she gave him a hug that said a "good-bye" in body language. Tomorrow would be another day and the day after would be another day and the day after that would be another day………………………

Years and years that dropped forever into eternity had honed the edges of Dakota Memory. Like the intensifying blizzard on that North Dakota night, an emotional storm charged through two physically separated minds that remained mentally together. Like an unrelenting wind that filled the cracks of time with nothingness, they reached for each other with empty arms.

MACK

Twisted mane hung with burdocks to the bottom of his neck. So entangled was his foretop that it protruded like a unicorn's horn. A semi-trailer backed toward the pen of killer horses. Some of them were frightened by the rattling sides of the old truck and started milling, jostling and charging. Mack stood completely still and watched. He had been a stallion for six years and had escaped both the knife and the emasculator. Small things like trucks didn't upset his psyche.

When he was three, a Rugby, North Dakota rancher had broken him to lead and then turned him out with a band of PMU mares that needed to be impregnated during the summer. He did his job. Mack was a genuine range stallion, a part of wild Americana. For the next three years, until the rancher died, Mack ran freely with his band of mares during the summer and was corralled with the other stallions during the winter. All of the breeding stallions were kept in a single pen during the winter. A small length of log chain was attached to one front leg of each horse to prohibit fighting.

Stallions placed together, to establish hierarchies of order, will bite with sharp teeth and kick with powerful hind legs to inflict great physical harm to their adversaries. Mack's fights were initiated by approaching his opponent with an arched neck and after smelling noses, he would begin screaming and snorting. Then, striking with his front feet, Mack quit playing mental games and began physical destruction.

The old rancher had the remedy for Mack's vicious fighting. The physically damaging aspects of stud fighting could be virtually eliminated if Mack was punished for every front leg strike. Mack, and all the other stallions, equipped with a chunk of log chain, were punished swiftly and severely by the striking of their own front legs. Fighting was disrupted at its earliest juncture. Thus, eleven weaker stallions and Mack lived with forced acceptance during the severe North Dakota winters. The pregnant mares lived from October until May in a long barn.

Inside the barn, each mare was equipped with a harness that collected her urine. Thus, the term Pregnant Mare Urine (PMU) was invented. Researchers discovered that PMU contained the female hormone, estrogen, useful in hormone replacement therapy for post-menopausal women. The rancher and his two sons had a large operation of 300 mares. Only those mares checked in foal, and guaranteed as such, could be used in the PMU program.

Mack had been selected as a breeding stallion because of his robust healthy appearance and his size. Most of the rancher's mares weighed over 1500 pounds. Larger mares produced more urine—hence more profit. One gallon of urine from a pregnant mare would bring the rancher more than ten times a similar quantity of milk from a dairy cow. Like Mack, all the stallions were vigorous breeders and sired foals that were hardy survivors and not overly large. The rancher's draft horse mares would give birth more easily if they carried foals from stallions smaller than themselves.

Mack looked to be only about 25% draft breeding. Judging from his deep liver-chestnut color and plain features, he was probably part Belgian. His distant parentage traced to highly domesticated Thoroughbred Remount stallions used for upgrading rancher's breeding stock and totally wild Mustangs that were escapees of the Spanish Conquistadors. For record keeping purposes, he was sired by and out of UN-KA-NOWN, old horse lingo for a horse whose pedi-

Belgian Mares, impregnated by Mack during the summer, used to produce Pregnant Mare Urine for medicinal purposes

Front view. Note the jugs used to collect PMU

Back view. Note the harness attached to each mare with hose leading to the collecting jug

gree remained forever a mystery. Born as a wild horse on the range, there was no way to ever discover Mack's parentage. Even though his lineage was unknown, an experienced horseman could easily spot the substance, speed and endurance that would make every work horse, race horse or wild horse proud to claim him as a descendent. Except for his head.

The mares loved Mack. Even during his rookie breeding season, as an immature three year-old, he was well developed sexually and could easily handle his quota of 25 mares.

During the summer of Mack's sixth year, the rancher, who had been in the PMU business for a generation, went to his greater reward in heaven. His large operation ceased and the auctioneer's gavel fell finally on each ranch item—horses included. Every mare "guaranteed in foal," was valuable property to be transferred to another PMU line.

The stallions went to the killer pens. This time, without the rancher's knowledge and the log chain, the stallions fought for temporary rights to strange mares that would never band-up with them on the North Dakota range. It didn't take Mack long to establish himself as king of the hill. His bold ruling appearance almost eliminated the need to fight for supremacy.

But no horse would reign supreme over the truck that was now parked and ready to be loaded with live horsemeat to be processed into small paper packages. The French would eat well.

Mack had never been in an enclosed area. His whole life had been spent as a wild range animal. Mack's beauty was undiminished by his unkempt grooming. No brush had

*Thoroughbred Remount stallion,
probable ancestor of Mack*

ever touched his chestnut coat that was the liverish color of black walnut wood. Nor would he ever desire that a curry comb or grooming instrument of any kind make contact with his tight hair coat.

Looking at him from head to toe as a horse show judge would, the first thing noticed were his eyes. They were small and beady, often squinting to obtain a sharper perspective. The rolling of Mack's head accentuated the white encircling his eyes. He studied every action. Except for the completely white sclera, the old-timers would have called Mack "pig-eyed." According to Professor Jessie Beery, founder of the Beery School of Horsemanship, Mack's small eyes indicated a bad disposition that would make him unpredictable and resistant to training. Mack had already proven that Professor Beery was right. Other animals knew him to be exceedingly treacherous and resentful. He would act quickly and with power at any attempt to restrain his will.

A bulge between his eyes extended upward and downward. As the killer buyer approached, Mack rolled his ugly head and pawed the ground. Mack's knot-headed attitude had saved his life many-a-time. His common face portrayed the confident alertness of an attacking mountain lion. Yet, he watched with rolling eyes seeming to be as instinctively evasive as the lion's victim.

Predators and their prey have different eye sets. Horses, like other victims of hunters, have eyes set on the sides of their heads. Hunter's eyes protrude directly forward from their brains. Mack's eyes had compromised the phylogeny of the hunter and the hunted.

Mack, like all horses, would flee when threatened. When escape was not possible, he would not submit and fought

Mustang mare with roan Appaloosa color, probable ancestor of Mack

Belgian work horse stallion, probable ancestor of Mack

with fury. His long, hairy ears flicked back and forth hearing every detectable sound and the nostrils of his overly large muzzle flared with each breath. Mack was sniffing the air, increasing his olfactory sensitivity by turning his top lip upward. His most primitive sense was highly developed.

Even the most incorrigible horse can be subdued and trained, but some are less domesticated by nature. Mack's head, according to some horse trainers, would make him almost impossible to train. Like Franz Gall, a phrenologist who lived in the 17th century, the old-timers in the horse world believed that the shape of the horse's skull determined disposition. Gall had stated that the protuberances on the human skull would actually determine personality and intelligence. People with protruding foreheads and large eyes were thought to have larger frontal lobes and therefore, greater intelligence.

Many horse trainers scoffed at the phrenology analogy. Even criminal behavior in humans was at one time thought to be evident on the person's face. Mack's head made him look like a criminal.

Mack's body made him look like an Olympic athlete. His neck was bowed and angular like an arch extending upward. When teasing mares before each breeding attempt, the juncture between his head and neck, his throatlatch, looked chiseled and clean. Wide massive shoulders with high withers at the base of his mane sloped with a long angle toward his heavily muscled forearms.

Mack's temperament was visible on the outside of his body. Any experienced horse trader could see his Thoroughbred breeding. The Remount programs of the United States Cavalry provided Thoroughbred range stallions to the ranchers of the Western United States. Pulsing blood vessels lay close to the skin. Mack's mustang ancestors were wild horses that had escaped from the early North American explorers into Mexico and The Louisiana Purchase Territory. His rock-hard feet were perfectly formed with open, elevated heels. The same Appaloosa colored mustang ancestor that gave Mack his white eyes had also given him iron feet with narrow stripes of white that ran vertically. The hoof provides support and in the wild, equals survival.

Mack's draft lineage gave substance to his speedy, durable physique. Had he been selectively bred in Europe, his breeding would have been called "warm-blooded"—minus the feral component.

Thirty-two large horses, crammed body against body, were jolted into a balanced stance as the diesel engine jerked the loaded trailer away from the loading dock. All twelve stallions and twenty reject mares, not checked in foal, breathed rapidly with native fear. Wet flaring nostrils, steaming in the cool autumn air, created a small cloud around the truck.

The driver of the ancient semi jammed the highest gear. Mack was on his last journey. He was headed for France where it is said the enlisted soldiers eat beef and the officers eat horsemeat.

But France was a long journey from Rugby, North Dakota. The butcher buyer had an old trailer pulled by an even older tractor. As Jack's fate would have it, he broke down close to the ROCKING J just outside Harvey, North Dakota. The horses had to be unloaded in one of Jack's corrals for the night. That's when Mack became part of Jack's broncobuster history. Without hesitation Mack was purchased for a profit large enough to pad the killer buyer's pocket and pay for the overnight use of Jack's corrals. As the repaired semi bounced over the potholes of the ROCKING J with one less horse on board, Mack's ultimate destiny had changed. So had Jack's.

The next morning, Mack was gelded. Stallions are a nuisance and resistant to training. Their unpredictable nature and constant obsession with teasing mares and fighting geldings, makes anyone knowledgeable about horses want to change their minds from "ass to grass." Forty feet of one-inch rope was used to physically subdue the six-year old rank stallion. Two free rope ends were looped around his hind pasterns and attached to a knotted portion that had been made into a collar around his neck. Two of Jack's strong ranch neighbors threw their muscle and weight into the free ends and snatched Mack's back legs off the ground.

Mack hit the ground with a rolling thud. After a fruitless scramble, Mack's back legs were pulled toward the collar and fastened with half-hitch knots. Mack was, for the first time in his life, 100% submissive. Jack castrated most of the stud colts in his locale and was known for his sharp-knifed expertise. But Mack was not a young colt. He was an old stag who had been breeding mares for four years.

Jack had little experience gelding rank stallions like Mack, but knew that, once on the ground, the big muscular horse would be as helpless as a heavyweight wrestler on his back. Mack's testicles would be well developed, easy to find and quickly excised. This time, Jack was wrong. Mack was a high flanker. One of his testicles had not descended and would require the services of a veterinarian. For the time being, Jack would remove the one large, descended testicle and let the vet complete the surgery at a later date.

The surgery done, Jack hit the half-gelded horse with the knotted end of the rope. Mack jumped to his feet. "Perfect. That'll draw the cords back and make him heal faster."

Hardly a drop of blood was spilled and Mack jogged to the hay bunk to start eating. Jack pulled his shirtsleeve across his sweaty forehead and proclaimed, "That only changed half his mind from ass to grass. We need to get the other testicle out as soon as possible. He'll still be rank with one testicle. High flankers as old as Mack never drop their testicles. They're meaner than studs and can't get a single mare in foal. I'm surprised Mack did so well breeding mares with only one good testicle. He must really have a high sex drive."

By morning the blood on Mack's hind legs made crackling noises as he walked a little more bowlegged than usual to accommodate the brown, crusty soreness between his thighs. Although he walked a little short behind with his head hung lower, his little pig eyes studied every movement of Jack's twirling lariat. Born on the range he had learned to be watchful and to learn from experience. Constant, instinctive vigilance was his best friend. Living for another day depended only upon his personal savvy.

The testosterone in his bloodstream would not quell with the removal of only one testicle. Riding high in his flank, where even the best horse doctor would be challenged to locate and excise his remaining manhood, was another undescended spermatic cord and artery that remained completely attached.

Jack limped on his left leg as he walked in a circle around his new half-stud. Mack's beady eyes squinted to the point of near closure never permitting the man who had castrated him to disappear from his visual field. The pair circled each other with some mutual respect until Jack tried to move closer. Snorting with fright and confusion, Mack reared, whirled and charged to the corral border slamming into the two-inch hardwood planks as his sliding feet plowed the slippery manure-sand surface.

Jack pursued the unsuccessful escape and with some reluctance, Mack turned to face his enemy. Quickly stepping back, Jack rewarded the horse for facing him. Gradually, Mack learned to look directly at his trainer and seemed to have learned that his survival depended on paying attention to the whip that cracked in Jack's hand. If Mack showed even the slightest indication of running away, Jack began repeatedly cracking the whip. The sound of the whip made a noise like a tree branch cracking over his head. Being instinctively afraid of such sounds, Mack would do anything to cause their cessation.

Soon the horse seemed to be under some sixth sense control. Jack was smart enough to allow Mack to escape or avoid anything aversive if the desired response was emitted. Within minutes, Mack was responding consistently to Jack's arm movements. By extending a left arm the horse could be turned one direction and the right arm did the opposite. Mack followed Jack around the corral with an invisible string tying the pair with a psychological knot. It was like a mental leash.

Dust blowing down the ROCKING J driveway powdered the corral and spooked Mack from his training submission. The invisible string broke. Jack's whip training had been overridden by the noise of Stretch's truck. Being a horse and not a truck-driving human, Mack didn't care about the age or condition of Stretch's rickety truck. Fenders flopped with no tailgate to hold together the rust of 15 salty winters. The hood was sealed next to the cab by duct tape and steel poked like tiny spikes from bald ten-ply tires. A fifth-wheel plate in the truck bed was attached to the truck's almost substantial frame. Mack passed no judgment on the beater pickup. Nor did Stretch.

What scared Mack was the dust and noise. Three-quarter tons of mufflerless engine snorted from the old corn binder and after the flopping driver's door slammed shut, a really tall guy climbed to the top board of the corral fence and sat down beside Jack.

Stretch blew a long monotone whistle that gradually gave way to an exclamation. "Dat's som kin a hors yu got der Jack! How yu plan on brakin im?"

Jack's shirt, peeled off because of the August sun, was tied around his waist with the sleeves in a double knot at belt level. Summers of sun had darkened Jack's upper body in a tanning parlor the size of North Dakota. His rippling body was only one shade lighter than his russet colored Hereford saddle and his face was one shade darker. Sun never touched his Wrangler covered legs.

"How about that body? I bet you never saw a horse built like him before? Look at the size of that gaskin muscle. I bet he could back fast enough to jerk the head off a steer." Jack kept facing Mack at all times while talking to Stretch.

"Gittin my traler al fixt up fer da col weder. Jus had ta tak som time off ta see dis som bitch. Jeez he's da bigst ridin hors I evr saw. He mus be som plow hors breedin too. I bet att assole'd buck a guy off as wel as see im." Stretch whistled again.

The crack of Jack's longe whip caused Mack to blow snorts and a grinding of teeth could be heard across the corral. Mack's broodmare band hadn't been ruled by an old wise mare like most bands. His harem members, including their offspring, were always under his control. He had no plans to change a successful strategy. The proof was on his body. No fresh bites marked his hide. One large fissure on his neck, covered by scarred hide and no hair, told the story of his herd supremacy. When Mack was only three, a rival stallion made the mistake of trying to steal a possessed member of Mack's mare harem. Mack's victim didn't know that he would rather sacrifice his body than lose a fight. Unchallenged, Mack had walked confidently through the rest of his stallion life. Until Jack.

"You get the first ride on him as soon as I catch him." Jack laughed as he cracked the whip.

"I ain't ridin att outlaw. Yu jis go hed an kil yerself ifn yu wan to. But I ain't gonna. Hors lik att needs ta hav his frikkin hed cut off. Why yu want im anyow?" Stretch turned with a fake move to leave the corral.

"Just look at him. That's the best looking horse in North Dakota since Illusion died, except for his head. Illusion had a good head that made him look intelligent. Can you believe those beady little pig eyes? And how about those long hairy ears? Not to mention that bump in his forehead right before his Roman nose starts. I never saw a better-bodied horse. I never saw an uglier headed one either. But like my dad used to say, 'You don't ride the head.'" Jack rationalized.

"Besides, he's kind of a challenge." Jack told the real reason for buying Mack.

Mack retreated to the farthest corner of the heavy planked corral and looked against the sun. Chestnut sparkles, deepened by his liver color, were like magnets attracting the whinny of an in-heat mare from the next pasture. Mack's entire body shook as his stallion reply rushed with a charge of air up his heavy larynx.

Primeval mating invitations fascinated Jack, "I bet Mack's inviting her to his place and saying he wants to buy her a card or get her some chocolate or a dozen roses. Or maybe he just said, 'I've still got the real thing baby.' As soon as I can get hold of that other testicle we'll get the rest of the testosterone out of his system. Then, he'll forget about that mare. I'm starting to work with him tomorrow. His serious education is all planned in my mind."

Mack galloped back and forth against the solid hardwood fence sliding to a stop at each end before rolling back over his hocks. The smell of the ovulating mare swelled within his olfactory bulbs and his animal brain interrupted any logical synapse that his ancestors might have treasured as they evolved.

WRECK

Through the barn window, August morning light, made uniform by a cloudy sky, barely made the cobwebs visible. Jack, startled as he hit one, brushed off the dust and continued past the double work horse stall throwing open the split barn doors to provide more natural light. Mack was in a box stall at the opposite end of the barn. Before beginning a potentially dangerous activity, Jack always tried to imagine possible outcomes and reflect briefly. He needed to completely clear his mind.

The cobweb had frightened him too much. He walked slowly to the work horse stall and reviewed his plans for breaking Mack. He looked for a lemon. There was no lemon slice in either the feedbox or the manger.

Musty hay with grayish dust covered the bottom of the manger. There was a rectangular feedbox in each corner with a two-inch hole in the top plank. The stall floor was built of railroad ties and the sides were of rough-sawn oak. A single heavy pole down the middle was hinged at the front and suspended from behind with a ceiling rope. Frayed ropes, that had stood the test of many halter pulling horses, were permanently fixed to the manger holes by knots that had been pulled tight so many times they could never be opened. Bull snaps, with rusted shut triggers, joined the one-inch ropes to heavy leather draft horse halters that looked to be 13 years lonesome for a horse's head.

The unoccupied double stall, used for Jim Steele's last team of Belgians, was crusted over and mummified. Protected from all the elements, it was preserved by Jack as a monument to his father. No horse would ever set foot in that stall again.

As Jack looked at the stall he remembered the time Doc Newton visited the ranch to treat the bigger, right-hand horse for her foundered feet that were sore and nailed to the floor with pain. The mare had gotten loose during the night and had eaten freely at a pile of shelled corn. By the next day, Old Dolly was standing with her front feet extended forward so her back legs could bear most of her weight. After the veterinarian explained the treatment, which was to apply heat to the foot soles so the blood flow would be increased, he taped a half-inch block under each front heel to create more pressure on the blood pumping structures of the foot. The frog and heel bulbs, like return-pumps, would send the stagnant pooling blood back to the refreshing heart. Jack's dad led the mare to the heating manure pile where she willingly stood for three days. Old Dolly knew what felt good and her acute laminitis never became chronic. Jack had learned to always listen to Doc Newton.

After treatment that day, Doc got started telling tales. He told an interesting story of how the word "lemon" became a symbol for inferior merchandise. Whether true or false, it was fun to hear this 75 year-old horse doctor tell stories. It seemed that, in former times, when horses were used for farm power, an occasional lemon slice would appear in the manger or feed-box of a newly purchased horse. If a horse trader wanted to get rid of a horse with a draining nose, often caused by an infected tooth, he would simply place a slice of lemon up the horse's nostril. In addition to being a natural sinus inhalant medication, the lemon would temporarily block the draining mucous and the horse could be passed off as normal. When the lemon dried it would drop from the horse's nostril and the horse's new owner, noticing the sick horse's nasal drainage and the lemon in the feedbox, would exclaim "I really bought a lemon this time."

Thereafter, Doc Newton claimed, all bad purchases were called "Lemons."

Jack was starting to wonder if Mack was a lemon.

As Jack approached Mack's box stall a loud snort blew from between the steel grates and as the door slid open, the half-gelded rogue retreated to the back of the stall with his hind feet aimed at the entrance. In nature escape is best, but with no flight possible the other option is to fight. Cracking the longe whip a first time, Jack entered the stall. The second crack, aimed more accurately, burned the horse's legs. The third crack hit nothing. Mack had quickly learned to evade the stinging whip. The face off had begun.

Whip breaking horses was one of Jack's specialties. Jack watched for the very split second Mack made an approach movement. The flick of an ear or the turn of an eyeball would terminate the continuously occurring aversive stimulus. Through association, the sight and sound of the whip would eventually substitute for the sting. By inches, the untrained horse became conditioned, like a B.F. Skinner pigeon in a cage, looking for a better way to survive captivity.

Shaped from turning to approaching and then following, in some primitive way, Mack had learned. Even without human touch, Jack had given Mack the magical power to turn off something that instinctively irritated him. One observation that Jack made of Mack's reaction to the whip training process was troublesome. It seemed that Mack rapidly learned to survive the moment, but he didn't seem to be permanently convinced.

Mack, like any wild animal, learned to escape and avoid quickly. Talking softly and offering the food-deprived horse some strands of timothy hay, Jack moved closer. Squinty eyes that narrowed at the corners followed every human movement. Mack's long hairy mustang ears flicked from front to back as his nostrils poured hot lung breath over the Dakota Colt. It was time for a noon break.

Jack hadn't thought of himself as a football hero in a long time. Now he needed every bit of athletic talent that he had ever possessed. He felt lacking—and insecure, too many linebackers and too many horses.

Sliding the stall door closed, Jack rationalized that he had done enough with the outlaw and that another day of food and water deprivation would further soften the horse's attitude. Really, he didn't want to be alone just in case something happened. If only his father or Uncle John could help. But the team of draft horses and Jim Steele were only Dakota memories. Uncle John, in the local nursing home, was a victim of too many horses like Mack. He had broken many, and some broncos, after they exited the railroad cars to North Dakota corrals, had broken Uncle John.

And Danni. Danni Penfield. Where was Danni now that he really needed her?

As he reminisced, he could still see his father's large left hand with one finger missing. Around noon he would use it as shade for his eyes when gauging the sun time. Then his browned face and wind-burned lips articulated that always-welcomed phrase, "It's time to put on the feed bag." Jim Steele told his son the expression traced to another era when work horses toiled in the fields and were fed in canvas bags instead of feed boxes. Jack's dad concluded, "No matter how busy your Grandpa Joe was, he always gave his horses a noon break. And Jack, we could always catch the lazy ones on Sunday because they knew they had the day off."

He remembered living with Uncle John for the last two years of high school and that Uncle John used the same "feed bag" expression. The only difference was the food. Made bachelor style, it lacked considerably of spices and was mostly flavored with salt and pepper.

Finishing his warmed-up soup, Jack submerged specks of pepper that hadn't mixed with other ingredients. A few stayed on the surface. There was no visible pepper in Danni's cooking.

Jack almost felt guilty about Mack's one-gutted appearance and leading him from the stall he told his neighbor Stretch, the trailer dweller, that today was the day. All the preliminary training had been done and it was high time to cowboy-up and ride. Mack had been sacked, saddled and thrown. He had been haltered for days and had stood tied with only half rations. Exercise and dieting outlined Mack's muscles making him look like an equine anatomy chart.

Jack led Mack to a round corral that was used for breaking horses. The seven-foot high walls provided complete visual isolation, suitable for beginning training. Jack knew that the round pen would not control extraneous olfactory and auditory stimuli.

Minutes after Jack's foot slipped into the left stirrup, Mack was loping circles in the round pen. This was the horse Jack had always wanted just for himself. Now, Jack could actually feel the speed, coordination and strength that every athlete recognizes as the known elements of any great performance. With Mack's UN-KA-NOWN pedigree Jack could make no estimate of other factors such as disposition, trainability and endurance.

In a few days, the round pen seemed too small for the shrunken 1200 pound horse. He had lost fifty pounds, and his body, that was naturally like hardened steel, now looked to be further tempered by exercise. A full ration of oats filled his tightened stomach.

The one remaining obstacle to training was the testosterone that still fed Mack's libido. One remaining epididymis was still attached to his high flanking testicle. Mack's stallion snorts and striking front feet kept Jack watchful.

Stretch swung open the round pen gate. Mack and Jack scouted the expansive Dakota horizon filling their eyes with a thousand acres of harvested wheat fields. Jack chirped and squeezed his legs. Mack moved willingly forward into the wide openness and the smell of the ovulating mare. She had listened to Mack's greetings and waited for the feel of a real stallion.

Mack broke into a crooked gallop as Jack fought with both the herd instinct and the horse's lack of training on the straightaway. Mack held his pig-eyed head high in the air, as his gallop changed to a charge. He smelled the horses beyond the wheat field. His lungs were still full of air and without any hesitation he bellered a mating call that shook his whole saddled body. Without asking for Jack's permission, or responding to the cues of his round pen training, Mack made a beeline for the herd.

Jack, being an experienced horseman, pulled on the left rein to turn the runaway horse into a spiraling circle. He remembered his father telling the story, time and time again, about being nearly killed by a team of horses that bolted when he was raking hay with a dump rake. Jack, for the first time, realized the terror his father must have felt as he clung to the rolling harnesses trying to balance himself on a four-inch hardwood pole that separated the galloping 1500 pound broncos. Jack visualized the huge feet missing his father's head as he bounced to the stubble of the hay field and could hear his father's screams of pain as the rake teeth became entangled in his clothes.

Jack's muscles strained as he pulled the left rein. There was a sudden pressure release that threw him backward against the cantle, as his left fist uppercut to his chin.

With the left rein broken, the next best solution was to try circling to the right. Mack's neck was of iron. Pulling seemed to have some effect and Jack, with a trainer's reflex, hauled harder with the whole length and strength of his lithe body.

Jack knew that when things go wrong there was a big space between what he knew should be done and what actually could be done. That time was at hand. He would just have to suck-it-up and take the punishment.

His brain flashed and he could almost feel the pain as his pony stepped on his four-year old feet and his father telling him to stop crying cause that happened to all young cowboys and that he better get a lot tougher if he wanted work with horses for a living.

But Mack was no pony and maybe the memory of his smashed left foot was just a premonition. Mack's slowing speed seemed to advocate the crude one-rein training. Jack's two hundred-pound wide receiver frame, which had only slightly filled out since playing football at Nebraska, surged with adrenaline. His whole body reeved against the horse's neck muscles causing the saddle to twist by the pressure of Jack's foot in the left stirrup.

His surgically mangled football knee, with no remaining cartilage, pressed bone against bone and Jack hardly knew that his foot had slipped through the left stirrup. The realization upon him, he whispered in a strain-strangled voice *"Jesus."* Jack wasn't sure if he was swearing or talking to God.

Breaking colts on the ROCKING J was risky business and Jack's horse training trophies were not standing on some fireplace mantel. He wore them on his body. But Mack wasn't a willowy yearling that would easily submit. In the middle of the unfolding wreck, Jack remembered first looking at Mack's head, a dictionary picture of bad disposition. Why did he even want to mess with this horse? Mack's incorrigible attitude made Jack's decision seem both stupid and self-destructive. Jack was trapped. Trying to jerk his foot from the left stirrup while still pulling the right rein caused his body to turn across the top of the saddle until his left leg was wedged through the left stirrup—to the bottom of his knee. The ache in Jack's knee multiplied into agony and was then suddenly gone. Jack knew he was experiencing physiological shock.

Jack's life-saving responses were becoming incompatible. Some things weren't—like Danni and him. Danni's mental image survived in Jack's brain despite her physical absence. Remembering Danni's description of being knocked out while jumping her Thoroughbred, Jack became even more determined to survive his immediate predicament. Remembering the warmth of her body on that Dakota night, Jack was motivated to cling with even greater desperation to his Hereford saddle that was starting to turn sideways. The narrow stirrups, called "ox-bows," that had held his feet securely when doing ranch work, now threatened his very mortal existence.

Jack had never been dragged. But like every cowboy that ever climbed on a horse, it was his greatest fear. His dad made him ride bareback and his first pony bucked him off three times in one day. As his father's three-fingered hand comforted Jack's child injuries, he explained, "You hardly ever get hurt bad by falling off riding bareback."

Jack was stuck in his own saddle. He was beginning to panic.

Images flashed in rapid sequence through curled bundles of neurons that could remember things quickly and clearly like pictures and songs and words that people said and how he felt at certain times and how people touched his body and heart but not how logic would do it and he saw his mother's and father's casket and he wondered why he thought of Mom first when he used to hang around Dad most and he felt guilty for not spending more time especially with his mother and then saw the twisted metal of the car wreck and heard his own voice promise Uncle John to preserve the ranch and he saw the dead body of Illusion being pulled by the neck with a lasso choke hold by a single harnessed work horse so that he could be skinned out and sent away for tanning so he could be hung on the porch wall and he still swore that no one would know the real story behind Illusion and he heard Stretch telling him what a mean bastard Mack was and he tried to repent for thinking the word "bastard" and he saw Curly's head looking at him with those real glass eyes not the kind that are called "glass eyes" or "watch eyes" that are really blue eyes and what about those wall-eyed horses whose yellow eyes are the same color as their yellow bodies and he needed to quit thinking about horses and get tough right now to save his life and one of his college coaches yelled in his ear to "get tough or go home to North Dakota" and he got tougher but he didn't want to be tough all the time and there was this woman that really loved him when he was both tough and sensitive and he could see her wanting his manhood and asking him to come to bed by holding back the covers and showing him she was naked and he could hear the blizzard outside the window and feel the comfort of her breast against his face before he fell asleep and then Uncle John knocked on the door and they had to chase cows for the rest of the night and the woman he had been sleeping with made good food and put her warm hands on his cold cheeks and the whirr of the snowmobile engine and her touch and he wanted to say her name out loud but couldn't say it right now because he was too out of breath and besides he couldn't think of it anyway right now not that she needed a name because she was really the only woman he had made real love to and The Barbie Doll and Irene and a couple high school girls he thought he loved for a few seconds weren't even in the running with the woman whose name he sometimes almost couldn't remember because it had been so long but whose name he couldn't ever forget because there was no time left for him to think and he knew he might die in the wreck that he was in the middle of and wanted his last thoughts to be of the woman with no name and then he remembered her name and it looked to be five letters long and was kind of a guy's and then he got mad at her father not for naming her Danni but for splitting them up and he knew that son-of-a-bitch wouldn't be in Heaven even if he was going to Heaven after Mack killed him and he knew Danni would be there so it wasn't so bad to get killed and besides he could see both his parents and he wondered if Danni would find out about his funeral and when he thought about the flowers he knew it was time to get organized and stop this stupid crazy no-mind sub-cortical life going before your eyes bullshit and get back to trying to save his life no matter what Mack tried to do.

As Jack saw the ground coming up to his face, his logical brain kicked away the streams from his lower mind and shoved them back into their primordial residence. Jack remembered the solution. An old bronc twister had once told him that, if he ever thought he was going to get dragged after getting hung up in a stirrup, the only way to survive was to roll face down. That would cause his leg and boot to turn completely over in the stirrup. Then the stuck foot could simply slide out of the boot. Sometimes, the boot would also slide free. An exercise rider at one of the local racetracks, whose break-away stirrup didn't release, had been dragged around the entire track and suffered massive brain trauma. He barely survived and now lived in a residential facility for traumatically brain injured patients.

Jack would have probably avoided a similar fate if he had not gotten blind-sided by the cow kick of Mack's hind foot. That ended Jack's chances of making any further Earthly brain choices and started the streaming of the sleeping parts of his spirit brain that were on a one way horse express to Heaven.

Rolling his belly like a sunfish jumping from lake- water, Mack stretched his writhing body and snapped with a final twist that turned the weighted-leather sideways. Jack hung helplessly unconscious as the turned saddle strung the weight of his body between Mack's slashing hind legs. Like a bouncing muskmelon Jack's head hit the harvested wheat turf that was autumn dry and hard. Scrambling like an amalgamated egg, his asleep cortex jerked with each bounce trying to loose itself from the stalk of brainstem containing the vital centers that controlled breathing, blood pressure and heartbeat.

Drainage ditches that were watered only by flash floods separated the wheat stubble. As Mack's charge slowed to leap from one ditch-side to the other, his left hind foot smashed against the left fender and slid down to the stirrup that was still fixed to his unconscious passenger. Stepping solidly on Jack's left leg, Mack's 1200 pounds elicited a solid crack that was the fracturing of bone. A split-second later, a slapping sound, that was the slipping of leather, released the stirrup with its fender and leathers. Then, Jack and Mack parted ways as a broken Blevins buckle dropped anonymously between two yellow rows of wheat stubble.

Homogenized with trauma, Jack's brain had no eyes for seeing. In self-protective fashion, he lay breathing quietly and steadily and did not witness the terror that would have been the unfinished ride.

Two hundred pounds of human flesh, still attached to six pounds of boots, Wranglers and shirt were left in the rising side of the ditch attached to three pounds of stirrup and fender. Released from the greatest weight handicap that his ancestral remount breeding prescribed, Mack accelerated, not bothering to kick at the saddle that had turned completely under his belly until it began grating his flank. As the saddle slid backward, the one remaining stirrup slapped randomly against the cannon bone of his right leg. The mild punishment changed his head dives and hind leg kicks into a screaming charge. Like a medieval jousting stallion, he was searching for a suicidal spear on which to eviscerate himself.

Leveling off into a straight run, the pasture mare came into full view. With her scent shooting up his nostrils, the sexual area of his hypothalamus stimulated his male hormones. Mack had become more animal than animal. His roaring larynx rushed hot breath through his deep bass vocal folds and at the other end of his body, the testicle riding high in his flank descended into the scrotum to the limits of its shortened spermatic cord and artery.

Five barbed wires, erected with steel posts, were alien features in Mack's free world and the receptive mare on the opposite side of the fence invited his aroused libido. As the wires separated chest flesh, the popping sound of post clips holding barbed wire to T-posts, frightened the pasture horses.

Mack's final shriek changed to a grunt as a steel post entered his thoracic cavity. Forced by his combined weight and speed, the T-post drove into his intestines like a bending seven-foot bullet until it could no longer hold 1200 pounds of horsemeat and saddle. Crashing to the ground in a tangle of wire, the top three feet of steel post, coated with blood and guts, made a right angle bend. With a sucking sound, Mack's remaining momentum drew the fence post from his body. Then he fell free to the inside of the fence.

Intestines dangled with the Hereford saddle as Mack attempted to stand. An empty puff of cheek air was the only stallion scream that came through his lips. His diaphragm had been punctured. Now his bellering had no substance as his largest breathing muscle refused even a quiet nicker to call the pretty sorrel mare. Mack had sacrificed his life for her companionship. Collapsing fifty feet into the pasture, Mack expelled his blood-reddened intestines that strung behind his body like lines on a roadmap directing curiosity seekers to the tale of his death.

Before the late summer heat began decomposition and the maggots started to swirl his red, high protein meat into fly eggs, Mack lifted his head for just one last time to see the approaching mare. Her flaxen tail was raised and she lowered her head to touch Mack's nose, now unresponsive and closing in death. Only a few galloping strides before, Mack had screamed lusty greetings. When she turned to reveal her receptively swollen vulva, Mack's cooling nostrils barely twitched. Then she left. Another stallion, beckoning from the Dakota range, would be the sire of the sorrel mare's next foal.

Soaked with dried blood and intestinal fluid, Jack's Hereford saddle still clung to the dead, half-castrated stallion. Only the left stirrup and fender were missing. And Jack.

AWAKENING

After the darkness came a shining slim light beam like a flashlight looking down a tunnel with no end and a huge bright light with circles coming toward his face in the shape of sunflowers like the ones that hang before harvest one after the other and each one getting larger until it came directly at him and went into his being and the sunflowers disappeared and the brightest light he had ever seen opened into the endless tunnel and he could see his father at first walking toward and then mounted on his favorite horse the one made into a horse robe that hung in the porch and Illusion looked even more gorgeous than ever and the black leopard Appaloosa was prancing as a young half-broke colt and the horse was wearing the old R.T. Frazier highback saddle from the ranch house stair railing except it didn't show any scuff marks.

His mother was beside his father and they looked like newlyweds and his father's cut off finger was whole.

A young woman with dark hair smelling like shavings and with a strong build was with them and he wondered if it was Danni but it wasn't so he said hello to his folks and they all hugged but their mouths moved without words like they really weren't people and when they embraced there was only air to hold because there was nothing inside and they all laughed at the way they used to be with destructible bodies and said it was better to be like this without aches and pains and always youthful and having the love of God always with and never needing to eat or drink and everybody was happy and it would be this way for ever and ever.

And he tried to find out if Danni had arrived and they were sure she would come later but didn't know when because she was still busy taking care of sick people on Earth and she was really good at it because her father had died and she was trying to help everybody so they didn't come here and then they all laughed with souls of silence and because they knew this was their everlasting home they also knew Danni would be here shortly at least in eternity terms.

But Jack insisted that he wanted to see Danni right now and The Really Tall Guy said that the only way to see her was to leave and come back later and then they could come back together or as close to it as a couple could that is if he could find her when he went back to Earth so Jack was faced with a decision that was easy to make because he knew now where he would go when he really died and that once he found Danni he could come back after they had lived in their Earthly bodies which they had never really gotten started with because Danni had to leave to help her dad and he was assured by The Really Tall guy who seemed like God but was only his messenger that Danni wanted to see him on Earth before she saw him in Heaven and that he would always be welcome when he decided to come back so he went back to Earth.

When he left the comfort of Heaven, the sunflowers started to disappear and the bright light grew dimmer. The awakening came slowly. Jack knew he was alive, but couldn't completely open his eyes. At first, only something was happening and nothing was specific. The bright light was fading............distantly disappearing as though it wouldn't come back. And then, the light turned black.

Jack was saying good-bye to his parents and his father reached out to shake hands. Now it seemed like the cut-off finger was cut off again. And when he looked it wasn't his father's hand and the woman in white wasn't his mother. She looked like his mother when he was sick, when he had to stay home from school or when he went to the hospital.

Jack felt really confused and kept trying to get out of bed, but he was weaker than anyone could imagine the Dakota Colt to ever be. The sides of the bed reminded him of being kept in a box stall and his wrists were strapped to the railings like a horse tied to a manger. A Really Tall Man beside the bed kept saying something about how lucky he was and that he should thank God that he was tough and that the Blevins buckle was weak and broke before he was dragged very far. And then, he knew The Really Tall guy was just Stretch and not one of God's messengers. Jack's own consonants sounded of indistinct utterance and he tried to tell Stretch to talk more clearly, but when Stretch moved his mouth, the words didn't sound like real speech—only garbled nonsense syllables.

Jack quickly passed through the stage of confused agitation.

By early October, Jack had traveled from the deep sleep of September to purposeful and appropriate behavior. He was alert and well oriented enough to recall past events. It was more difficult to recall recent events, but aided by multiple therapies, his comeback was nothing less than miraculous.

The only blank space in his memory was The Wreck. Jack couldn't understand what had happened. He remembered riding Mack from the round pen and recalled the frantic gallop as he charged toward the mares. Then everything was blank and black, except for the bright light.

Stretch, his loyal companion, had a flexible schedule and stayed with Jack almost day and night. Upon the Doctor's request, Jack's really tall friend provided stimulation that helped to restore Jack's memory. Stretch's familiar face helped fill a void created by the hind foot of Mack.

Stretch told Jack about The Wreck. "Da las I saw yu was goin hell bent fer eleksion cros da weet field an haulin on da lef rein. Den I saw yu purtneer fall off cause I tink da rein broke an den yu was pullin da uder way an it seemd like yu was goona to be aw rite cause Mack kep slowin down. Nex ting I saw was yu draggin on da groun wid Mack runnin like a crazi maniak. I don kno how far yu was drug but it mus-a-bin bout a football field. When I got der yu was gone but yu was breathin OK and da stirrup was stil on yer foot witt da hole fender stil hookt rite on. Lookt like da Blevins buckle holdin da stirrup leather to da saddle was gittin ole an it gave out frum da pressur. Yu bettr tank God att ting brok."

Stretch went on to describe how he had loaded Jack in his old pickup and brought him to the hospital. Jack had suffered a traumatic brain injury and the doctors thought that Stretch should stay by his bedside until he woke up. "Day sed yu'd praly be OK ifen yu woke up agin, but I din't tink it'd tak att long fer yu ta cum to!"

In his back-forty hick cowboy twang, Stretch told about Jack's first awakening. "Wen yu wok up yu was perty groggy and da docters askt me to go wid yu to dis plase wher yu can git fixt up som mor. We'r in Red Wing, Minnesota now. An in case yu ain't got it figgerd out yu ain't in da hospitl nomor. Dey call it a rehab centr. Kinda like a long stayin hospitl wher dey speshlize in helpin people dat git hert in da brane."

Jack asked Stretch about what happened to Mack. "Wel yu see he din't kno much bout fences made a wire an he hit one a dem steel posts an drov it inta his belly jus bak a da belly buttn. Dare was guts strung out cros da groun fer a bunch a yards an at da end of da trail was Mack. Deader dan a doornail."

Jack tried to find something positive to say about The Wreck and told Stretch, "At least we don't have to take that other testicle out."

Stretch reassured his buddy that his Hereford saddle had been cut off the dead horse. Then the rendering truck with its emotionless cable wrenched Mack's gutless body into a whole truckload of lifeless critters. Jack visualized his child pony being pulled by the neck. Tears chilled his cheeks.

Stretch reached over to wipe the tears and said, "Hell, he was jus an ole outlaw. You don't need ta feel bad fer dat sombitch."

Jack's voice, weak from disuse, quavered more than usual when he told about his pony. Tagging on the last phrase he explained, "I guess you don't know that, when I first got Mack, I thought he was the reincarnation of Wildfire. He was the greatest, but he died too."

Stretch stood quietly alongside the rails of the hospital bed and didn't say even the first word because he knew what was coming next. Whenever Jack got in one of his nostalgic moods, which occurred quite often since the accident, he always started asking for Danni. Partly because of his brain trauma, Jack would begin to cry as he wondered out loud, "Where's Danni? She said she was going to visit her sick dad and I expect her to call or show up any time now."

Then the mood would pass and coming back to the present, Jack, looking vacantly into the ceiling lights, could recreate the sunflowers. Recalling the words of The Really Tall man, he gathered all his strength and sat vertically from the waist up, looking directly at Stretch. Then he said something that even Stretch didn't understand, "You promised that I'd get to see Danni if I came back to Earth."

Jack noticed candy stripes of red and white that ran up and down. A red belt encircled her waist. Calling the young girl to his bedside he asked, "Have you seen Danni? My friend Stretch doesn't know her and can't seem to get hold of her. You're pretty and look like Danni. I bet you know her because she's a doctor. If you get her on the phone, let me talk to her. Or maybe I could have some paper to write her a letter. I wrote her a letter a long time ago. She never wrote back."

The candy striped girl and Stretch went to find the head nurse. "Ol Jack he jus keeps askin fer dis gerl dat he sez is Danni. An he seems mor seeryus evertime. I tink we need ta do somting bout dis."

"OK, let's go talk to him and see if I can make heads or tails of what he's trying to say." The head nurse was taking charge.

"Well, you see, I knew this girl just a little while ago back in college and when I was asleep they told me that if I decided to come back that I'd get to see her. This Really Tall Guy that looked like God promised me that Danni would be here. Now where the hell is she?" Jack's traumatic brain injury was allowing him freedom of speech, like an exaggerated First Amendment.

The nurse, who thought that Jack was demonstrating an emotional reaction to his altered neurological status, tried to appease. "Jack everything is all right. We know that you only have one living relative and he's in a nursing home. His name is John. He's your uncle. There isn't anyone you know by the name of Danni."

"The hell there isn't!" Jack grabbed the side of his bed and tried to stand upright. "She was just here and I could feel her holding my hand. Besides, I came back here only to see Danni. I could have stayed with my mom and dad and Illusion and the Frazier saddle. I want to talk to somebody about finding Danni."

Jack's demands only became stronger as the day progressed. His speech, although rambling, seemed to make some sense and the nurse summoned a speech therapist. Ms. Johnson would attempt to decipher the underlying meaning of Jack's emotional outbursts.

Ms. Johnson took a chair next to Jack's bed and calmly reflected the nurse's previous conversation, "I guess we need to talk about someone called Danni. Can you tell me about her?"

For the first time, someone was willing to listen as Jack explained. "Well, back in college, Danni was my girlfriend and she even went to the ROCKING J with me and helped in the blizzard. Then we went to town on the snowmobile and saw............ The Big Dipper and the next morning she went back 'cause her father had a heart attack. Then I never heard from her until just last night when this Really Tall Guy that looked like God told me that if I decided to stay alive I could see Danni. He promised me. Now I want to see Danni."

"What about the Big Dipper?" The therapist had noticed the hesitancy in Jack's speech.

"Jesus! I didn't think anyone was ever going to understand. Danni and I looked at stars after we got home on the snowmobile and I can't even mention what happened the night before the storm. Why didn't she ever write or call or come and see me? But a promise is a promise and damn it, I'm going to see her now come hell or high water." Jack's lack of inhibition following his accident was clearly understood by Ms. Johnson who had great success working with TBI patients.

Speaking in therapease Ms. Johnson tried to lead Jack in a positive direction. "Danni must have been a wonderful person. Was she real or is she someone you just imagined?"

"Real? You frickin' right she was real. She was the best looking woman you ever saw and she didn't have to dress up all fancy or put make-up on to make herself look pretty. And she could ride a horse better than most cowboys that were born on horses. She had dark hair like you and could do twenty push-ups. I know about being an athlete 'cause I played football. I used to have lots of women hanging around me until my knee got hurt. Then it was 'see ya later alligator.' My nickname was The Dakota Colt."

"You're kidding. You were that famous Nebraska wide receiver?" Ms. Johnson had done her homework by thoroughly reading the file labeled: **Steele, Jack.**

His reply, triggered by lobotomized-like liberty told the whole story of his athletic life, his family life and his love life. Actually his brain trauma, that resulted from being dragged by the half-emasculated outlaw horse, caused his verbosity. Ms. Johnson understood the nature of TBI. She listened.

With his catharsis complete, Jack turned to clutch his pillow and curled into as much of a fetal position as his left leg cast would permit. Pressing his face against the white fabric, Jack whispered, "Danni."

"I guess my report will conclude that Danni is a real person. We'll try to get hold of her. Maybe we can check with the doctor that was here to see you last Friday. She seemed real nice and they said she took a personal interest in her patients—particularly you. She usually comes once a week or so. Her name is Dr. Penfield. I think her first name is Danni too, so you two should really get along." Tired from his two hours of diagnostic therapy, Jack had fallen asleep before hearing Ms. Johnson's conclusions and the name of his lost Danni. Danni Penfield. Dr. Danni Penfield.

REUNION

It was Friday afternoon and for the nth time, Danni turned off the divided highway at Zumbrota, Minnesota. In the past four years she had visited many of the head trauma patients in Red Wing and it was becoming almost a routine. Today she had been sent on the mission again because, as her supervisor said, "Here's a head trauma patient you might be interested in Danni. I know you like horses. This guy got dragged by a horse and is in Red Wing. Why don't you run up there and check this guy out and present this case to the younger residents on Monday?"

The September sun was on vacation and the intermittent windshield wipers hesitantly sloshed one more swipe of drizzle as Danni pulled into a parking space reserved for doctors only. She reasoned that an umbrella might look fashionable, but would be more bother than it was worth. Just because she was now a fourth year resident from The Mayo Clinic didn't mean she had to be presumptuous.

Danni's high heels evaded each rain-filled sidewalk crack and approaching the front door, her left foot slipped, nearly spilling Danni and her briefcase. Regaining her composure, her stride quickly gained the hallway lined with residents in wheelchairs. She always made a point of smiling at each patient. Before reaching the nurses station, Danni stopped to talk briefly with a young man whose twisted face couldn't even say, "Good afternoon Dr. Penfield." His outstretched hand grabbed her wrist and with guttural, unintelligible mouth noises pleaded for this white-coated person, he knew to be a doctor, to make him like he used to be.

"Would you please find the chart of the horse accident patient?" Danni asked the charge nurse.

"We were expecting you. The chart's right here. I guess a crazy half-castrated horse bucked him off and then the horse dragged him by the left leg. His leg got pretty mangled and it's still in a cast. He's still unconscious, but seems like he's starting to respond to some stimuli. He's in room 321," said the helpful nurse.

Danni responded with detachment, but intellectual understanding, "Those horses can sure be dangerous. A horse cold-cocked me too. And that was just an ordinary tame riding horse. It sounds like this guy was riding a lunatic."

Dr. Danni Penfield arrived at the patient's room before looking at the chart and she almost collided with a really tall guy. Tipping his new cowboy hat before he left, he apologized, "Scuse me purty lady we don't wanna hurt Docs att look like you. Din't I see yu here las week wen I waz wheelin my buddy ta da windo?"

Danni smiled and couldn't help remembering the personality and speech of the really tall guy with the new hat. "Yup, yers truly is back agin." Danni had practiced her lingo.

"Wel I hope yer a good ma'am docter cause da Colt iz shur wantin ta git better. He keeps tryin ta wak up an kan't git it done. Yu git rite in der an halp im now an dats an order ta a docter not frum one." The really tall guy stretched his long legs into a five-foot stride as he headed for the cafeteria.

Danni had heard the word "Colt" and quickly diverted her glance to the name sign on room 321. It said, **"Steele, Jack."**

She quickly opened the chart to find out if her best dreams and worst fears were being fulfilled. She had always wanted to be with Jack, but not like this. Tears blurred her vision and blotted the first page descriptives:

Age: 29
Permanent residence: Harvey, North Dakota
Closest relative: John Steele
Parents: James and Anna Steele (deceased)
Education: B. A. University of Nebraska
Hobbies: Horses, football
Marital Status: Single

With all her training about being objective—yet sensitive— Danni could not maintain her composure. She walked quickly into Jack's room and shut the door. Then, she completely fell apart. Her pounding heart and out-loud sobbing seemed so loud that she thought someone might hear the commotion. Danni dropped to her knees beside the bed and begged God to heal the man she had always loved.

Danni remembered how their first date had been a ride in her little pickup and how Grandpa loved him too. Jack had watched her ride. Later, she forgot his gloves. If only she hadn't forgotten the gloves. Jack's hands were cold and he needed them to warm his hands. Bending over the bedside, Danni lifted both of Jack's arms and after holding them for only moments placed them under her white coat next to her breasts. Danni whispered, "Jack. Jack Steele. Jack Steele I love you."

As she held his hands, Jack's arm muscles tightened and he seemed to be trying to shift his weight. Danni could feel that the calluses on his large hands had softened. Jack's sun-tanned face had faded, and the muscles of his once strong arms had atrophied. He looked so fragile, so vulnerable.

Danni stood up and walked to the door, placing a chair in front of the doorknob so it couldn't be opened without warning. She needed some time to be alone with Jack. Then she walked back to his bedside. This time she would try to act like a real doctor, like Dr. Danni Penfield should. The light she shined into his eyes only slightly constricted his pupils. A new wave of emotion swept over her as she saw his eyes like the first time she saw them dilated. Only this time his pupils were widened with the memory of pain and not the anticipation of pleasure.

She jerked with convulsive crying, like a child who had just lost a parent at the county fair. Although she knew the very essentials of existence, she felt totally helpless. There never is a good time or a good way to lose a loved one. She had always felt that her life and Jack's were synchronized, even when they weren't together and that if he died or stayed in this semi-life state, she would never be the person she aspired to be.

Just above the cast on Jack's left leg, Danni could see the scars from the Dakota Colt's reconstructive knee surgery. The Lincoln newspapers were right. His left knee had been damaged badly. She said to herself, "That's good Danni. Get it together. You won't be able to help him unless you do."

Danni remembered how she had tricked her father into meeting Jack and how The Dakota Colt's athletic ability and intellect had impressed even her father. She regretted the way her father had disapproved of their relationship. Seeing Jack like this, she empathized with her father, as he must have clung to his wife's image through Danni's existence. The mother she had never known and the father she had tried to please, grieved her heart and stabbed at her stomach. Like a twisting knife wound to her belly that twisted harder and harder, it hurt so much that she needed some supernatural force to remove the blade. Worst of all, Jack was now gone. Even when they were physically separated, Danni felt they were together in spirit. Now, Jack's spirit was gone too.

Danni knelt beside Jack's bed for a second time. This time it was not from the weakness that grief brings, but to search for strength. Whether to God or Medical Science, or both, she began praying. She asked for Jack's smile like when they danced after the blizzard. She asked for a chance to bury her head behind his strong shoulder on the way home. But most of all, she asked to be able to stand with him on a cold North Dakota night with her arms inside his snowmobile suit. And of course, she asked for The Big Dipper.

Danni questioned her own words as she talked to a supernatural power that she wasn't sure existed. Besides, any God that did exist would think her prayer too childish. The Big Dipper belonged to all God's children—not just Danni Penfield and Jack Steele. So she made one more prayer request. "God, please help Jack wake up."

As Danni removed the chair from the doorknob she looked in the mirror and saw her red eyes and swollen face. Now, without Jack's spirit, she felt completely alone and before leaving his room, returned to Jack's bedside for a third time. With the door wide open, she stood holding his hand for the longest time, squeezing and massaging with the complete intellectual understanding that Jack didn't know she was there, but with a new feeling of hope that her spiritual awakening would move throughout Jack's cold hands. "God, please help Jack. If you do, Dear God, I'll pay you back by taking a more genuine interest in every patient."

For the first time, it seemed that Danni was seeing clearly the multiple factors that had altered her existence and all the reasons she had become a doctor. It was as if a veil had been lifted and she finally understood her title of "Dr. of Physical Medicine and Rehabilitation." Some things beyond medicine are mysterious and the unknown forces that bring miraculous recovery, though difficult to comprehend, must be acknowledged.

For one last time Danni squeezed Jack's hand and hearing footsteps coming down the hall, dropped his hand and picked up the chart. The really tall guy stood in the doorway with his head nearly touching the top of the door jam. Knowing that Jack didn't have any living relatives other than Uncle John, she asked, the gawky, pigeon-toed cowboy, "Are you a friend of Jack's?"

"Yup I'm his neighbor. Me and Jack work tageder on brakin horses mostly. But he got tangled up witt att damn Mack. Yu tink he's gonna be awe rite? Yu shur waz in here a long time. Mos docs jis kinda come an git rite-a-way. But I kin see wher you'd like dis guy. You know he's da Dakota Colt doncha?" Stretch rattled on.

Danni smiled weakly and for her own reasons, not wanting Stretch to know more about her, reached out and shook his hand. "Take good care of your buddy—and thems Doctor's orders."

At Zumbrota, Minnesota Danni's car joined in a Friday evening exodus of bumper to bumper traffic. She knew that Jack was a strong man and that the prognosis for recovery worsened with each day of coma. Danni also knew that she was a Doctor of Physical Medicine and Rehabilitation who had the highest level of training in helping patients recover from TBI.

Danni couldn't wait to tell the first year residents what she had discovered. She knew they would have difficulty understanding. With the benefit of her enlightening emotional experience, they too might just have a chance to become better doctors. Therefore, she made up her mind to tell the whole story. She felt a reckless freedom and a need to make a late Friday evening sermon to the other residents.

What differentiates great doctors from merely good doctors is more than knowledge and ability. It is also the ability to truly empathize. Her life's path and focus had been forever altered in one chance meeting with a head-injured cowboy from North Dakota who used to play football and majored in Philosophy.

It was like Intro. to Soc. all over again. Danni wondered out loud, "How many chances....?"

Early the next Monday morning, a portable beeper signal interrupted Danni's meeting with the residents. She was giving another sermon related to her Friday experience. And now, she had two more large chunks of data since she had visited Jack on Saturday and Sunday as well.

She excused herself and reached for the nearest phone. "You've got an urgent call from a guy in Red Wing, Minnesota with a funny sounding name like Scratch or Stretch or something. Do you want to take the call or should I have someone else handle it until you're done with your presentation to the residents?" queried the receptionist.

Danni choked her words into the phone, "I want the call and I'll go to my office. Transfer the call there."

Danni left the residents to their own amusement. This phone call was hers and no one else's—and not just professionally. A lingo familiar from just three days before rattled the receiver, "Is dis Docter Danni Penfield? My friend here is wakin up frum bein asleep fer bout over a month an he keeps askin fer you an sez stuf kinda crazi like som really tall guy att lookt like God sed you'd meet him here ifn he cided to keep alive. An he keeps tellin me att somebody was rubbin his arm tryin to wake im up and he gissed it wuz an ol gurl frien and dat id be you Doc Penfield. Can yu mak heads or tails a dis stuf? Did yu go ta skool in Nebraska? 'Cause he sez dat yu are shur gonna be late fer Soc klass taday. An he gits real mad sometimes an we add ta strap is arms down ta keep im frum gittin ornry—speshly wen we tol im att you weren't ere. Yu know anythin bout dis stuf?"

Danni's reply was crisp and short. "I'll be there in one hour."

The phone clicked before Stretch could say, "Tank yu Ma'am Docter."

Taking only time enough to transfer required duties, she dismissed the residents saying with both exhilaration and reservation, "That horse accident patient is regaining consciousness and I just have to be there to help the staff."

Dr. Danni Penfield arrived in tennis shoes so she didn't have to watch for the sidewalk cracks. She hustled for the entrance, not taking time to greet any patients or even stop at the nurse's station.

Good ol reliable Stretch was standing by Room 321 and asked, "You bak agin? I spekted Doc Penfield not yu. I'm gittin kinda confused. Which Doc are yu?"

Danni smiled, "I'm Danni Penfield."

Stretch's surprised reaction was cut short by a raspy voice from the hospital bed. "You're already late for class. Come here and sit by me." Hearing Jack's atypical voice, Danni's eyes filled and before Jack could notice that she was crying, she reached over the bed railing encircling as much of his head and chest in her bosom as the posture would permit.

"Damn," said Stretch, "I nevr saw no Doc do att befor. I giss I'm excess baggidj an yu two need ta be rentin a room or at leas be alone fer awile. Com an git me wen yer dun."

Danni had a dual duty to perform. While she conversed with Jack as a friend, she attempted, as a doctor, to evaluate his neurological status. Compared to only three days before, the pupils of Jack's eyes were now reactive, his muscle tone had improved, his skin color was brighter and his smile was symmetrical. Now, she also noticed that he wasn't paralyzed. Most importantly, he was awake and fully conscious.

She promised herself that this time, before she left Jack's room, and everyday thereafter, she would get down on her prayer bones to thank—not ask.

On the way out, Danni explained to the charge nurse that Jack Steele was recovering nicely and that she would personally be providing Jack's treatment and on a daily basis. She said, "I'll be here everyday until he's ready to go home. I'll juggle my schedule at work and will, absolutely, fit Jack's rehab in, even if it's late at night."

The leaves fell brightly colored, torn at the stem from their mothering branches. Soon only the tough red oak leaves remained. Jack grew stronger. By comparison to his pre-accident status, Jack's sense of humor, depending on the situation, was unique, improved or impaired. To Danni, his loss of inhibition almost seemed like a blessing as Jack, for the first time since college, vigorously pursued her and demanded their togetherness. That pleased Danni. Years of thwarted and suppressed feelings now found free expression. Jack's mind had been shook loose from stifling precautions. If Danni arrived late, Jack would tell Stretch to call her at home or at the clinic or do whatever it took to get her.

The sun of late October radiated through the Bronco's windows. Danni flipped off the heater switch as she drove around the Red Wing area looking for rehabilitation sites suitable for Jack's carry-over program. He needed something that was stimulating, yet protected. On Highway 61, just south of town, she found the perfect spot. The sign read **Hiawatha Valley Ranch.** Two life size plastic horses, wearing authentic bridles and harnesses, were hitched to a stagecoach as though waiting to load passengers. Only a thin layer of unmelted snow on the stagecoach roof hinted that the Hiawatha Valley Stage Line would be a little late today. Danni knew how Jack would appreciate this cut of Western Americana.

Nancy Berger's white blouse had blue colored Arabian horses galloping around the entire front and with sparkling eyes her friendly, "Hi. How are you?" told Danni she was in the right place. Sitting squarely on Nancy's head was a white felt western hat that looked like it was being worn for the first time. With Nancy sitting behind the cash register the stomping of boots was followed by the appearance of her husband Norm.

HIAWATHA VALLY RANCH
near Red Wing, Minnesota

*Sign noticed by Danni while looking for a
carry-over rehabilitation site for Jack*

*HIAWATHA VALLEY STAGE LINE, looking
life-like, waiting for passengers to board*

Danni quickly studied the western shirt and jeans that the ex-cowboy wore. His breathing was labored and in her mind, Danni correctly diagnosed his disease as some form of asthma such as "farmer's lung." His wrangling days had been terminated. Leather boots, worn smooth with soles tipping sideways, made short quick steps toward her and when he got within about five feet, she could see the character of his western hat. Sweat stains darkened its naturally gray color to almost two inches above the sweatband. Lifting it off his head, Norm asked with a slight twang, "Is there somethin we can help you with young lady?" The word "young" confirmed Danni's original hunch that she had found the right location for Jack—and herself.

Supper at Jack's residential facility concluded at 6:30. Danni teased Jack's curiosity by mentioning the western store she had just found. Jack swung his legs over the side of his bed and said, "Let's go."

Jack insisted, in his new free speaking style, that he would rather walk than ride in a wheel chair. "How in the hell am I going to get better if I can't walk? I can't break colts in a damn wheel chair."

Assisted by Danni on one side and his aluminum cane on the other, the three of them reached Danni's Bronco. "Jesus! This sure is a lot fancier truck than you had at Nebraska. I can still see you taking off from my ranch in that little pickup. I watched until the snow from the plow made you disappear." Jack twisted his face and turned away from Danni to hide the painful Dakota Memory. His leg hurt too, but the thought of Danni leaving him for all those years was too tough for Tylenol #3. Jack wept more openly than Danni had ever seen and she knew that his tears were caused by his recollections. His TBI simply allowed a freer expression of the pent-up emotions.

Norm and Nancy Berger, proprietors of
HIAWATHA VALLEY RANCH

Franklin fireplace at HIAWATHA VALLEY RANCH,
a cozy setting for Jack's rehabilitation

Danni knew for sure that Jack's crying was not an expression of emotional lability. She had felt the same. But her crying was done. Jack had not seen the tears Danni had shed as she prayed for his return to consciousness. Danni had kept her promise. Every day she dropped to her knees and thanked God for Jack's life.

Norm threw a piece of split birch on the fire causing the crackling of dried white bark. It was almost nine o'clock and Jack had swapped enough stories to make up for at least one week of the four he missed during his coma. With an audience of five gathered close to the winter warming fire, Jack entertained by describing both the remembered and retold portions of the Mack wreck. He concluded, "It was the scariest ride I ever had and I've ridden some bad horses. He was one confused and sex-crazed son-of-a-bitch and when the rein broke, there wasn't really anything to do but get hurt. Getting dragged damn near killed me. The good thing is, I don't remember even hitting the ground. I must have gotten knocked out right away. Thank God that Blevins buckle broke."

Standing to leave, Jack's right hand curled around his curved aluminum cane top. By using it on the right side his Physical Therapists had taught him to employ the cane as a fake leg. His cane became his right leg and his right leg became his left leg. Thus, his damaged left leg could heal and gradually regain strength as it assisted and eventually took over for the cane. Jack hated his cane, but he hated wheel chairs even more.

"Young fella, I got something you might be interested in. Just sit down for another minute and I'll get it." Norm returned a few minutes later and with his bifocals, read an inscription that read like a prescription, "For old and hurt cowboys."

Jack examined the black walnut cane. Sanded and buffed completely smooth, Jack's hands ran over the liver chestnut surface. A sapling had been twisted and then sculpted. Following the blackish-red heartwood of the little black walnut tree was a continuous white stripe that wound with its invented turns. Just beneath the bark of every precious black walnut tree is a thin layer of contrasting white.

Carved on the crook was a Merry-Go-Round looking horse with his neck bowed around the curve. On the end of the crook was a horse's head. With open jaws and long hairy ears pinned against his poll, the beady-eyed monster looked like the devil's reincarnation of Mack. "Except that he's a little darker chestnut, this looks just like that bastard that almost killed me. I'll take it. And don't tell me the price 'cause Danni's buying it for me." Jack reached out with his new cane and tapped on Danni's purse.

"You don't owe me a thing." Norm countered "Except when you two kids decide to get married I get to come to the wedding."

Danni blushed and Jack, standing only on his good leg, picked her off the floor and pretended, with hopping steps, to be carrying her over a door threshold.

"Guess I still need that thing," Jack puffed as he leaned on his new cane to end his superman demonstration. "But I'll guarantee you, I won't use this damn cane one minute more than I have to. I hate this thing already. I'm not being ungrateful you understand, but the minute I can get along without this damn thing, it's going to burn in hell like that bastard that tried to kill me."

The very next day Jack drove Danni's bronco back to The Hiawatha Valley Ranch. He also insisted that she not be a back-seat-driver. "Just 'cause I'm a little brain damaged and can't get around, except with this fancy cane, doesn't mean I can't drive."

Norm's greeting helped Jack convince Danni that driving wasn't all that tough. "Hey, young fella, I guess you got that Bronco broke. She sure drives like she's broke to neck rein and turn on a dime short enough to give you five cents change."

"Piece-a-cake!" Jack bragged. "But I came back to see some more of your museum. Maybe I could even find some loose change to buy something for the ranch. You know I'm going home pretty soon. I just told Stretch he can go home tomorrow to fire up the ranch so we can start breaking the colts by Christmas."

"Hey, I got a saddle you'd really like. It ain't that old, but it's a pretty sucker. Lots of silver all over and it could be used for either an investment or keepsake. If you can make it upstairs, we'll look at it." Norm led the way up a steep flight of stairs stacked with hat and boot boxes that made the stairway as narrow as it was steep. Jack, using his springy right leg, hopped up the stairs and didn't bother to use his cane or left leg.

Danni followed closely behind and when she saw the russet-colored saddle with all the silver, she put her head on Jack's shoulder. Remembering the Frazier saddle at The ROCKING J, Danni burst into unrestrained crying, "Jack you've got to have that saddle to go with the Frazier. I'll pay for it. I know Norm won't overcharge you and we'd have a mate for the one on the stairway at home." Danni didn't even notice that she had used the word "home" to refer to Jack's ranch.

Norm described the terms of the agreement. "Tell you what. I ain't getting any younger and could use some money, but this saddle is special to me and I'd like to see it go to the right people. I'll just sell it to you 'cause I like you. I can't carry it down stairs 'cause of my breathing and Jack can't cause of his leg. Young lady if you can get that saddle down the stairs without killing yerself, you can have it fer just what I paid fer it over ten years ago—$5000.00. I'll even throw in that new cinch on top just in case you ever decided to ride in a parade or something."

Danni lightly touched the polished sterling silver and wrapped both hands tightly around the solid steel horn. Then she promised, "We'll take care of your saddle Norm. It'll never leave the family." This time she intentionally used the words "we" and "family."

Norm yelled down the stairs, "Get the coffee pot on Nanc, we got a deal to finish by the fire."

Seated around the Franklin fireplace, Jack and Danni listened to a story that Norm had never told to anyone except his closest friends. "Well anyhow, I first saw that saddle right after I got out of the army in 1945. There were big parades all over the United States and the soldiers that lived through World War II were having a good time. At one of those celebrations in Iowa County down in Southeastern Wisconsin, there was a fella riding a golden palomino, all decked out with that saddle hanging across the horse's withers. I tried to buy the saddle, but Mr. So and So, 'cause I don't want to say his name for reasons you'll hear later, said he got it from his father-in-law and wanted to keep it in the family."

"This isn't an X-rated story is it?" Jack pretended to be embarrassed and Danni gave him a shot in the ribs with her elbow.

"Let Norm tell the story so we'll know the whole truth about the saddle." Danni exited the conversation.

At that point Nancy picked up the tale. "Norm saw that saddle lots of times and every time wanted to take it home. Then, forty-three years after he first spotted the saddle, the owner called saying he wanted to sell it."

"Yup," Norm continued, "But he wanted $5000.00 and I didn't have that kind of cash. Well I consulted with the boss," Norm winked at Nancy, "and got the go-ahead from her to try to make a deal. I ended up trading a bunch of using saddles and a couple of old highbacks plus $1000.00 in cash. Two months later we made the last cash payment and Mr. So and So dropped off the saddle."

"Here comes the juicy part." Jack had anticipated correctly.

"When the guy walked through the door I hardly recognized him. He used to be a big stout man, but he had shrunk with cancer. He told us that he only had about a year to live and the only reason he wanted to sell the saddle was because of his children. They were already fighting over it and he didn't want to go to his grave with a family feud on his mind." Norm acted like the story was complete and rose from his chair to put another split chunk of oak on the November fire.

"But that's not all," Nancy intercepted Norm's fire tending. "Tell what happened the next year."

With the triangular wood chunk as his pointer, Norm punched the last lines of the story. "The next year a lady called me and wanted to buy the saddle. I told her that it wasn't fer sale. I bought it fer my museum and planned on keeping it. I never bought it to sell. Then she asked if she could borrow it to use in a parade. I smelled a skunk under the woodpile and knew I'd never see my saddle again if she used it."

"Yeah, and she didn't even own a horse. We found out later it was Mr. So and So's daughter." Nancy finished the juiciest story part and then gave extra advice. "When you guys have kids I hope you don't have those kind of problems. The most important thing for parents to do is agree on how to raise the kids. Kids and religion and money, those are the only things that can interfere with a good marriage."

Danni blushed enough for Norm to see, "Nanc, don't be making this sweet young thing embarrassed."

Danni wasn't concerned about the provocative conversational topics. She was worried about telling Jack of the child he didn't know he had.

Flames changed with the varieties of wood from hot burning oak to fast burning box elder. Norm and Jack talked saddles and cowboys and even some about women.

Danni had retreated from the "man talk," knowing wisely that it was a great opportunity for Jack to become more independent. Besides, Nancy was directing her toward some gorgeous western outfits that would look good when she and Jack were two-stepping in North Dakota. She hoped the restaurant still had counter stools and featured spontaneous blizzard dancing.

Sterling silver parade saddlle, purchased by Danni to become a ROCKING J keepsake

The next day Stretch left for North Dakota. He would try to recoup what could possibly be left of the ROCKING J. He told Jack not to worry and he'd call. "You ain't got ta worry bout me cause I ain't gonna be ridin nun a em colts til you git bak to halp me. An yu git well. Them's Stretch's orders. An don't yu com bak to da ranch widout att woman. Yu did att once now damn it lern yer lessn. Besides we need a good docter up dare."

After Stretch's departure, Danni started asking Jack to do more things independently. One day Jack said to Danni, "Let's go see some horses or something. I think I could almost ride if it wasn't for this cast. I guess my head is healing, but my bad left leg is the worst part of my body, ever since it got wrecked in football."

On the way to visit a local riding stable, Danni told Jack about seeing his pictures in the newspapers. He couldn't believe that she had followed his football career right to the end. Showing Jack eight years of newspaper clippings, he responded with some vulgarity, "Jesus! You mean to tell me you made this scrapbook about me and we weren't even together? Why in the hell did you put this picture of me in here? That's not you I'm with. It's that airhead that thought I was God till I got hurt. I hope you weren't jealous of her. She was just a temporary convenience."

"And damn it, why didn't you call me and let me know you were still interested?" Jack responded further with his new brain released freedom. "Hell, I would have transferred to Northwestern to be with you and I might not have gotten hurt there. I told you that in my letter. And why didn't you write back?"

Danni was careful not to answer too abruptly or truthfully. She knew Jack's confused brain still needed to heal. She said only what was necessary. "I always loved you and couldn't forget about the blizzard. That snowmobile ride home, after we danced in the restaurant, was the most fun I ever had in my life."

Danni was still trying to conveniently tell Jack about their son. As they rode along a trail of colored October leaves, she thought of simply blurting out the truth. But she didn't want to spoil the moment.

The Hay Creek Trail wound its way through forests and across crushed rock roads that bordered a spring fed trout stream. Danni suggested that they let the horses drink a few gulps. Jack, with his impaired mobility, was riding a kid-broke 14-hand gelding that had seen better years. As he slid off his saddle, Jack landed in a pile of leaves and rolled into the water pretending to be hurt. Danni jumped off her horse to provide assistance and Jack tackled her as she came near. "It's a good thing we got these old gentle nags or we'd be walking back to the barn. I think the one I'm riding is old enough to vote," joked Jack with his grasp on Danni firm and unrelenting.

Crushing the oak leaves they rolled playfully on the river bank, neither thinking that one was a trained doctor and the other her patient. They were just Jack and Danni.

By early November, Jack was ready to leave the care center. Danni wanted to ask him to live with her, but still hadn't been able to risk telling Jack about little Dakota.

Jack rented a small apartment in Red Wing and continued to receive physical therapy for his wrecked leg. He was now able to walk with a cane and made it an everyday practice to walk to the local YMCA where he could be gently rehabilitated by swimming.

TOGETHER

An early blizzard blew into southeastern Minnesota. The school closings, announced on WCCO Radio, included every district in the Rochester area. Danni, scheduled to see Jack both as a patient and friend, was not able to get someone to watch little Dakota. The only solution was to include Jack's son on her 50-mile trip to Red Wing. Danni's four-wheel-drive Bronco had no problem with the snow packed roads.

Danni knew that Jack would be swimming at the YMCA and as the front tire contacted the Y parking lot curb, little Dakota asked, "Mom, why are we stopping here?"

"We have to go inside for a minute and then we're going to dinner with one of my patients," replied Danni. "And please refer to me as Dr. Penfield—not Mom—when this man is around."

Jack's cane barely touched the snowy sidewalk as he hustled to the Bronco. "So, who's this young football player?" Jack asked as he saw little Dakota. "Judging from your stocking hat, you must be a Minnesota Vikings fan."

At the "come as you are" restaurant, Jack and Dakota barely allowed Danni to talk. Before ordering, Dakota whipped out his football trading cards that he called his "Cardboard Legends." "Mr., do you know anything about football?" Dakota asked.

"Well, I used to know something, but my shot knee made me forget," Jack said evasively.

"Did you get your knee hurt playing football? That's what happened to my dad. He used to play football in college at Neb......" Dakota was interrupted by Danni.

"Let the kid talk. He's not hurting anything. What position did he play? I hope not wide receiver. That's what I did until the stretcher carried me off the field in Nebraska." Jack countered.

"Yup. That's what he was, a wide receiver. He played at Nebraska too. I bet you knew him cause he was real famous. They called him the Dakota Colt." Danni had given up on trying to stop the conversation.

There was a long silence as Jack looked across the table at Danni. "Well, I'll be damned." Jack knew.

Jack invited the pair to his apartment. It was Monday night and it was about time to educate his son on the ins and outs of football. Dakota didn't quite make it to halftime. Snuggled inside his sleeping bag, that had galloping horses on the fabric, Dakota conked out on the living room floor. Danni and Jack admired their son.

After Dakota was sleeping soundly, Jack reached for Danni's hand and led her to the next room. Without thinking, he forgot his cane and walked only with Danni's assistance. Seated across from each other, the veneer plastic on the top of Jack's apartment table was not cold enough to keep their hands from joining.

Jack's interrogation was both hot and personal.

"Why didn't you tell me about Dakota?" "What the hell gave you the right to raise that kid without me knowing about him?" "Would you have ever told me about Dakota if I didn't get my frickin brains beat out by that damn Mack? He's my kid too. Didn't you ever think about that? Didn't you ever think about me? Didn't you ever think about my feelings?" Despite his rising anger and lowering inhibition, Jack never disengaged his large hands from Danni's soft touch.

Danni's rationalizations followed. "My father was the whole reason that this ever happened. I understand that now. And I did try to contact you, but you always seemed to be doing something else or with some other woman. After my father died, my grandmother gave me a box of family valuables. That's when I found the letter you wrote. I could have killed my own father. He successfully kept us apart for all these years. When Dakota was born, my father treated him like the son he never had. I always felt obligated to my father for raising me all alone and when he was in his last years, taking care of him was almost a full time job. When I moved to Rochester, he died almost right away."

Even in his impaired condition, Jack could sense that Danni was about to crack. He reached across the table and extending the whole length of his upper body, placed a hand on either side of Danni's face. "Well damn it, your dad is dead now. He's not going to keep us apart anymore. And don't even think about keeping me from seeing Dakota."

Seeing Jack sprawled across the tabletop, Danni fashioned a half smile that seemed to only increase her apologetic crying, "I'm sorry for all the pain we've both experienced. Can you ever forgive me for being such an idiot?" Danni's apology seemed almost inconsequential as Jack slid back down the table. Balancing his left hand on the edge of the table to support the weight that his leg still couldn't carry,

Jack made two large steps before engulfing Danni deep within the crevasse formed by his outstretched arms.

"If I had only known. I would have been down to your place in an instant and your father could have just gone to hell." Jack whispered with raspiness and pushed his unbridled feelings toward Danni. As their bodies met full force, neither attempted to kiss the other, but both knew again the repressed pleasure of hard human contact. They pressed with greater strength, until their clothing seemed to separate them too distantly. The thumbnails of Danni's hands came momentarily to the front of Jack's large biceps and attempted to extract her entire being, both body and soul, from his physically demanding grasp. It was as though the grip of her hands told Jack what she really wanted. The deeper Danni's nails drove into Jack's biceps, the more aggressive were his demands.

As the pressure in Danni's hands went from her thumbs to her fingers, she could feel herself completely out of control, not caring about the consequences of her actions. With desiring fingers, Danni told Jack that she was ready. Fingernails from both of Danni's hands pressed grooves into Jack's triceps and she wanted to have him closer than even the most violent pulling on his arms would permit.

Jack's trembling anticipation only heightened Danni's arousal. Unable to locate the last button of Danni's flimsy blouse, Jack spilled it floorward with a wrist snap that left Danni exposed in her braless apparel. As Danni divided Jack's cowboy shirt, the popping rivets disconnected from each other in less than one second. Simultaneously removing their remaining articles of clothing, the bedroom of Jack's apartment seemed too far away. Years of animalistic desire had only been inflamed by the same years of intellectual denial. They crumbled into tangled action on the kitchen floor with their fevers blocking the linoleum- tiled coldness.

The river of lost years, swollen large by deprivation, burst through dams of inhibition and control. With love totally engulfing, only the most primitive expression of affection could quell the adrenaline that emptied bloodward as the combined actions of their bodies demanded emotional purging.

One last explosive lunge hammered their joint history of regret to passionate ectascy. No sounds came from either Jack or Danni's mouths except for the indistinguishable and inarticulate noises that arise from underneath brain parts where there is no reasoning and hedonistic pleasure prevails. Jack's muscles, exhausted from frantic action, froze in a few moments of autonomic tetany. Then they released his entire weight. Jack's body descended in total relaxation.

Danni clung in positive desperation, not wanting the muscles of his body to stop flexing so soon. She wanted more from the man whose seed had once made an internal life that was now half-grown and called Dakota Frazier Steele.

Before rising from a spontaneously made bed on the kitchen floor, Jack's lips, still warm with passion, passed one more time over Danni's mouth. Both his auditory and tactile senses picked up the spoken message that was now a totally intelligible utterance, "Jack. I need you, Jack."

Danni quietly assisted Jack to his feet. Slinging one arm over her shoulder, she transported him, like the injured football star he was, to his bedroom.

Dakota had peacefully slept through his parents' blizzard revival. Danni placed a warm kiss on her son's cheek and tucked a second blanket around his feet. The horses on Dakota Frazier Steele's sleeping bag pranced their way through his midnight dreams.

Danni decided to sleep on the couch the next time she visited Jack.

Before crawling into Jack's bed, Danni flipped the door lock. There was more lost time to catch up on.

Cartoon voices awakened Jack for the first time ever. Going to the living room, he found Dakota in a semi-stupor with eyes stuck against make believe. "I see you made yourself at home."

Dakota responded by only shaking his head. Jack didn't know first-hand about raising kids, but could tell that this moment was sacred for Dakota. They could talk and romp later.

The next few days, Danni was almost sorry that she introduced the two "men." They were so involved with each other that she got barely the slightest amount of attention. They played like two pups in the Minnesota snow. Jack was ready to go home.

Stretch turned Jack's pickup at the Jamestown corner. Like the loyal friend he was, Stretch had arrived to help Jack return to his Dakota memories. As they headed toward Harvey, North Dakota on highway 52, Jack asked to drive his aging pickup. Less than two hours later, the ROCKING J sign, swaying loosely from its cable suspension, dipped with a wind gust as though waving a "welcome home" greeting to Jack. "Boy, it sure feels good to be back home. I see the two year-olds are looking over the fence and there's steam pouring out their noses. They must be healthy. I hope you haven't started riding them. I can see the place where Mack started running away with me. Thank God I don't remember the rest of the ride."

"Yu jus beter tank God an da twelv disciples too dat yu ever cam bak ere at all. Yu one lucky sombitch. If att stirrup buckle din't brake yu'd be dead as att Mack who shovd dat steel post clear thru his guts." Stretch concluded.

Stretch brought Jack up to date on the recent ranch happenings. Then, like he always did, bounded out to his rust bucket and revved the engine through its gears before backing off at the end of the driveway to make mufflerless cracks as though they were departing gestures.

The stores of Harvey, North Dakota were stuffed with Christmas goodies to warm the hearts of the predominantly Norwegian and German descendants. Jack's mother always honored her Scandinavian heritage by rolling lefse into thin sheets and baking them on the cookstove. This year Jack was on a special shopping mission. He needed more than lefse.

Jack searched the jewelry store for Danni, the saddle shop for Dakota, the candy store for Uncle John, the hardware store for Stretch and the grocery store for everyone.

Danni and little Dakota cruised on Interstate 94 with the cruise control set at 80. As the miles wore down, Danni couldn't help but remember the first and only trip she had made to North Dakota nine years before. Crossing the border between Minnesota and North Dakota, the eight year-old product of her last visit pointed to a large sign and yelled, "Look Mom! They got my name on that big sign." The sign said "North Dakota."

The driveway looked the same. A large mud hole, that had stayed the same depth since the driveway was layered with gravel, was covered with snow that hid the underneath ice. A puppish looking Australian Shepherd still tried to bark Danni's Bronco away and when he saw little Dakota jump from the city slicker truck, the pup tried to lick the rest stop chocolate candy off the kid's face. His name was "Young Pal" or as Jack joked, "Dog." Jack still called his dog, "Dog." He nicknamed Dakota, "Kota," and Danni, "Doc."

Jack was outside doing evening chores and before he could reach the house, Doc and Kota had already ascended the wooden porch steps of the ROCKING J. They were fixing a pair of 20-20's on the hide of Illusion.

As Jack entered, Dakota exclamated his point, "Hey Dad! Mom says this horse hide is Illusion. He looks like a tiger or leopard. Jesus, he's really weird."

Danni, with pretense, put her hand over Dakota's swearing mouth. Since his accident, Jack didn't care and used a few extra cuss words himself, "You damn right he's weird and that's what made him worth so much money."

Inside, the ranch house looked different than Danni had remembered. Jack, unable to do much work outside since his accident, had taken to housekeeping and the house looked kept. The same roughly hewn kitchen furniture sat on wide varnished boards and the living room carpet had seen a shampoo machine within the last week. Natural pine aroma crowded the other ranch smells from the Christmas tree area. There was a large present wrapped in last week's newspaper with a twine string securing a careless wrapping job. A large cardboard sign stuck under a hand made safety knot, displayed the hand written name: DAKOTA. Another small "man-wrapped looking" box, with no name and a red ribbon three times its size, was restrained from tipping by leaning against Uncle John's candy box that wasn't wrapped at all. Stretch's present was in a heavy black case with a pair of leather gloves attached by a vise grips to the handle.

The gifts that Danni brought were all neatly wrapped with hand curled bows and properly taped corners. While it was easy to guess the contents of the presents that Jack had attempted to conceal, the valuables inside the Danni wrappings would remain mysterious for two more days.

"And Dakota, don't be peeking at what Santa, under the auspicious of Mom and Dad, brought you." Dakota already knew his mother's big words, though this time he might conveniently pretend to be hard of hearing.

Dakota went to sleep on Curly's back. His sleeping bag, decorated with galloping horses, provided the first equine company the old horsehide had known in more than a half-century. Dakota's pillow was propped against the horse's poll, located at the base of Curly's skull.

Shortened winter days made long nights and with their child safely asleep on the living room floor, Jack told Danni to get dressed in warm clothes so she could help him with some barn chores he hadn't been able to complete because of his still ailing leg. Before turning on the barn lights, a high pitched nicker broke through the dark. Snapping on the light switch Jack yelled, **"Surprise!"**

A chunky Appaloosa pony, covered with red spots and numbered tags sticking to the hair on each hip, turned to see his new family. "I just bought him yesterday. They had a special Christmas horse and tack sale at the Harvey sales barn. Do you think Dakota will like him?" Jack asked a question that needed no answer.

The morning of Christmas Eve, Dakota's new pony gave rides to both Danni and Dakota. The clicking of the camera did not frighten the gentle pony and the final picture was taken by Stretch, who had made his daily trip to the ranch to assist with the chores. With the foursome within the square of the framed image, one last click completed the film and Stretch handed the camera back to Danni. "Ma'am Doctor, yu beter git dis to da drug stor cus ther som pitchers att ar mity pleesin."

Green and red littered the living room floor and Curly could barely see the Christmas tree. But even though his make believe eyes were obstructed by wrapping paper, the bouncing of his once owner's great-grandson almost made him come back to life. With Curly draped over a hassock, the child's new 13" Hereford saddle was swung atop his withers. Mounted like a seasoned rider, Dakota cranked Curly's jaw sideways. Digging his new cowboy boots into Curly's flanks, the sleeping white horse's glass eyes seemed to sparkle with real life against the string of Christmas tree lights. Cracking his whip and nearly hitting Uncle John, Dakota froze momentarily in his stirrups and prophesized, "I'll be riding Conclusion like this pretty soon." Dakota had given his pony a name that sounded like Illusion.

All the presents had been opened except one—the smallest. Jack personally delivered it to Danni, but in typically male fashion had forgotten to include an appropriate card. Duct tape secured a large red ribbon to the tiny yellow box. Neat opening was impossible. There were two separate smaller boxes inside the already small outer box. Jack told

Danni which box to open first. Inside was a silver chain necklace.

Jack opened the smallest box and reaching inside, removed a smoothly worn ring with no adornments. The silver metal was discolored and thin.

Jack lifted the necklace from Danni's hand. Without speaking and with everyone watching, including Young Pal, Jack threaded the chain through the ring and hooked it around Danni's neck.

Then, Jack turned to the audience of three people, one dog and the red pine Christmas tree and made a small speech. "This was Annie Steele's wedding ring, my mother's. Nobody knows, but I kept this ring hidden for all these years. Now it's time the woman of the house starts wearing it again." Danni's tears exceeded her toughness.

Smoked curled from the ROCKING J chimney and the old cookstove's warmth spread through the vapors of onion smothered venison chops. The porch floorboards reverberated with the stomping of big, little, old and dog feet. Young Pal's alerted nose was first through the door. Dakota followed closely behind and as Jack reached out to hook an eight and one-fourth year-old leg, Dakota evaded Jack's cane with a scissoring leap. Uncle John smiled at the horseplay.

Except for the levity near the front door, the house was totally quiet. The three men, which was the company that Dakota wanted to be included in since coming to the ROCKING J, halted their goofball after-chores activities. On the kitchen table was a piece of white typing paper with oversized writing. It said:

*"You can't have food til you find me
And if you look real hard you'll surely see
A wrapping filled with Christmas glee
Hidden somewhere 'round the red pine tree."*

Young pal wasn't distracted by the note and stood next to the cookstove where the cooking fumes were the strongest. Jack's grin grew as Uncle John put his reading glasses back in his shirt pocket. Dakota didn't quite understand the note and Jack explained that it was a mystery that needed solving. "It means that we have to look for Mom before we get breakfast." Dakota grabbed the scruff of Young Pal's neck and fell backwards with the entire dog between his figure-foured legs. With one large squirm the pup spun loose and smacked saliva over the kid's face. Then the hunt was on.

It didn't take long until Dakota, with the pup's help, found a long, rounded and irregularly shaped package lying next to the Christmas tree. Red stocking feet protruded from one end and a white stocking hat from the other. The package moved. Attached was another large note that said:

*"To Jack, whose games I loved to see and play
A lasting gift for you to have on Christmas Day
It seemed so long and time is often far away
The mortal gift that's wrapped inside will always stay."*
danni

A 2:00 P.M., dinner reservation for three had been made at the only open restaurant in Harvey, North Dakota. Jack's pickup returned Uncle John to his nursing home residence. Danni waited at the ROCKING J for a few minutes after Jack left so she wouldn't arrive too early.

Danni stood looking at the unspoken symbol of the ranch and reached inside her purse for the developed pictures that Stretch had taken. She selected the best one and pinned it to the center of Illusion's back. Then holding her finger in front of her mouth, she said to Dakota, "Shhh, don't tell your dad I put this here."

"Can I write something to put up there too? Dakota's question was answered in the affirmative.

Seeing Dakota's message, Danni was greatly affected and spun around to walk toward her vehicle. With quick steps she left the sagging ROCKING J porch. Danni didn't want her son to notice the moisture forming in her eyes. After starting the engine and telling Dakota to "buckle up," Danni pressed hard on the parking brake and told Dakota, "I'll be right back."

Returning to the ranch house stair railing and the R.T. Frazier highback saddle, Danni paused to let her fingers feel the indentations that Mr. Frazier's stamp had permanently embossed on the leather. The remembering felt good.

Then Danni touched every sterling silver concho on Jack's newly purchased parade saddle. As her fingers caressed the saddle's silver, she looked at the wedding band encircling her right ring finger. Only yesterday she had removed it from the silver chain around her neck and now, she wanted more.

With decided intention she removed the ring, that Jack's mother had worn smooth, and exchanged it to her left hand. She paused at the protruding silver saddle horn to stroke its hard and shining smoothness. Danni was determined to return to the ROCKING J and complete her family with

Jack. Her only regret was that she had waited so long to make the right decision. Norm and Nancy would be invited to the ROCKING J for the baptism of their next child. She wanted Stretch to be the child's godfather.

"Hey Mom! Are you going to town or staying here to just look at the saddles?" Dakota was getting hungry.

Danni's Bronco wheeled her and Dakota directly to the front of a small establishment. Danni whispered to herself, "No wonder Jack wanted to come here for dinner. The last time we were all here I had just gotten pregnant. Dakota was less than one day old."

As her hand pulled on the door to break the seal between winter and warm, her memories of the Dakota night of nine years before stopped her step in place. Only the cold air rushing through the doorway snapped reality back to her brain and made it possible for her to take a stool chair at the counter.

When Jack arrived, Dakota was placed strategically between his parents to help change his 360-degree spinning to bi-directional 180-degree swinging. Danni remembered her grandparents using the same maneuver and as Dakota's legs bumped from Danni to Jack and back to Danni again, the touching connected the threesome with a human voltage. In fact, with the low winter humidity, a few clicks of static electricity were generated by the child's activity. It seemed like the right time.

Jack started slowly. Danni wondered what he was going to say. She did not interrupt. "There's something I need to talk to you about and Dakota might as well hear it now, while he's young. It's about Illusion."

Dakota interrupted the serious atmosphere as only a child could. "You mean the horse that turned into that weird thing in the porch?"

"That's right," Jack continued slightly more at ease after his son's punched-in comment. "Illusion was a great horse—one my father loved and my mother worshipped. They bought Illusion as a weanling colt and turned him into the greatest stallion this part of the country ever knew. I can still see my mother making out the ads for *Appaloosa News* and remember how impressed I was as a kid to see four pages of pictures of colored colts in the next issue. Mom took care of the advertising and sales. Dad did the training and shipping. Most of the offspring of Illusion were sold before the buyers actually saw the horse and when Dad would deliver them to their new owners I'd get to go along to keep Dad company. We'd travel all over the United States and Canada and when we'd get to the new owner's place, Dad always guaranteed that the horse was exactly as represented or better. We only took one back home and that was because the colt got all skinned-up in the gooseneck trailer gate."

The story stopped, partly because the waitress was bringing a mound of mashed potatoes in a family style bowl and a plate of beefsteaks cut from the best loins west of the Mississippi. Maybe the food made it possible for Jack to continue, "When Mom and Dad were killed in the car wreck, Illusion was nineteen years old. Uncle John and I were left to run the ranch alone. I was only a teen-age kid and Uncle John wasn't a spring chick."

"What's a string chick?" Dakota's mispronunciation sounded comical.

"A spring chick is young. When you get old like me and your mom you're not a spring chick anymore." Jack replied and seeing Danni's faked judgmental look, retracted the second half of the statement. "Well, on second thought, I guess just me and not your mom."

Then Jack got to the tough part of the tale that only he and Uncle John knew. "Losing Mom and Dad was depressing enough without anything else going wrong. That was a tough winter and one February night, a terrible blizzard blew in and suffocated about half our cattle. Uncle John and I tried as hard as we could to keep the cattle moving so the snow would get stomped down, but after two days we were exhausted and couldn't keep going any longer. The rendering truck couldn't even get to the cattle until spring and most of the cows that lived aborted their calves."

Jack's voice choked and the ambient noise of the restaurant partially masked his weaker consonants. "I didn't know it then, but I do now. I got really depressed. I just sat in the living room, staring at the TV. The chores didn't get done and I quit playing sports. Uncle John completely lost interest. The anguish was too much for us to take. We neglected everything—even Illusion.

One day I came to the barn and found Illusion with his head drooping and nearly dead. I felt so guilty because he hadn't been fed for days and at his age, it didn't take long for Illusion to deteriorate. I always thought he died from neglect, but maybe he was depressed too.

The shock was just too much. The loss of my folks, the blizzard, the cattle, the calves, and now Illusion. I remember that I went to the barn and screamed where nobody could hear me and then got down on my knees and prayed for the first time since my parents' funeral. I cursed God after they died and stopped praying all together. This time, I prayed that God would either take me or get stuff straightened out."

"That was on March 26," Jack's voice regained it's deep bass tone and rose above the Christmas party jitter. "When I went to the barn door it was like my prayer had been answered already. A newborn colt, that looked like Illusion, was busy taking his first meal from his mother's nipples."

"Well, right there I made a pact with Uncle John and God and myself that the ranch would be preserved no matter what. I went to the house and got the skinning knives and before Illusion had lost the heat of his living body, he was skinned out. We shipped him to Colorado to get tanned and when he came back, Uncle John and I decided to put him where we would always be reminded of our promise. Probably because of the guilt we both felt over losing all the cattle and Illusion, we shook hands and agreed to keep the reasons behind Illusion's death a secret."

Jack dropped his head to the counter top and surrounded his face with his arms. Dakota looked at his mother who was holding her index finger in front of her mouth to stifle any childish comments. "I still feel like I let my folks down. I've never told a single soul about the way Illusion really died. Even the neighbors didn't know. They still think he just died. They just wouldn't understand. Both Uncle John and I felt terrible—embarrassed and ashamed. It was a big, deep and dark secret. I killed the very thing my parents loved the most—Illusion. It was like I murdered Illusion—the treasure of the ROCKING J."

"But I guess you two are part of the family now and deserve to know the truth. Sometimes truth hurts so much." Jack, lifting his head and wiping the tear stains from the corners of his eyes, ended the story and looked over at Danni and Dakota who weren't saying a word. They would never again think that the hide was weird.

Danni's Bronco crossed the Red River and broke the Minnesota-Dakota barrier. The North Dakota branch of I-94 had drilled the last months of their togetherness into a small shaft that she kept open only for Jack. She would leave North Dakota with only one thought. With Dakota asleep on his own mother's lap, there was no question in Danni's mind that her thinking was 100% correct.

Next weekend she would return to North Dakota for one more time. Once more would be enough. She would stay. Danni simply needed to extract her belongings from her Rochester apartment and rent a truck that could also pull her Bronco back to Harvey, North Dakota.

Moorhead, Minnesota would not be too soon. Just across the Red River, Danni applied the brakes of her Bronco and swerved across both lanes. Leaving the engine running to keep the sleeping Dakota Frazier Steele warm, she jammed the emergency brake and sprinted with 40-yard speed.

Grabbing the telephone booth receiver, Danni dialed area code 701 and Jack's telephone number. "Come on Jack answer. Where are you Jack? Answer the phone." Danni let the phone ring and ring and ring...............Danni felt obligated to talk to Jack, just in case he didn't notice the picture on Illusion's hide, or in case he made the wrong conclusions about her leaving.

ILLUSION

Danni rehearsed the words she had wanted Jack to hear for nearly the past decade. "We're coming back to the ROCKING J. This time Dakota and Danni are staying permanently."

Danni had visualized Jack's singular return to his ranch. After leaving Uncle John at the nursing home and waving at Stretch's trailer house, there would only be one individual that would understand his return to busy days and lonely nights. But Young Pal was only a dog. Danni thought of making a U-turn that would bring her back to Jack five days sooner and if she could have, she would have. Instead, Danni would promise Jack that she would call him every morning before he and Stretch did barn chores and every evening when she returned from Mayo.

Young Pal was watching for Jack's pickup and when he spotted the truck, still a half-mile from the ROCKING J mailbox, he came bouncing down the quarter mile-long driveway. He met the pickup halfway and as Jack swung open the door, an arm full of puppiness jumped into his lap. Jack and Young Pal sat together. They sat for a long time. Dogs don't have to learn to be happy. They just are. Young Pal heard Jack making sniffling noises and pushed his cold nose against Jack's cheek while licking the salt-tasting tears. The dog's loyalty didn't depend on something Jack did or didn't do.

With the engine turned off, there were only three sounds in the North Dakota winter. There was the confused, joyous sound from excessive activity as last week's newspapers crumpled beneath the squirming pup who looked like he was trying as hard as he could to be human. He was bouncing happy to see Jack and sat as erectly as he could on the newspaper strewn pickup seat.

With his human-like pose, the pup panted the happiness sound that dogs make whether their masters are happy or sad. Eons of selective breeding had produced a quality called unconditional love. Young Pal loved Jack without trying. Dogs don't have to learn to love. They just do. But Young Pal was just a dog. The only person who had enough positive regard to be Jack's counselor was a dog.

Crumbling newspaper, laughing Pal panting and Jack's crying, there were only three sounds in the Dakota evening. Jack sat, alone and lonely, on the cold and torn vinyl bench seat of his aging pickup. In the midst of Pal's laughter, Jack cried.

Time condensed into mental fractions as Jack pondered his history and predicted his future. Once again he was totally alone. Danni left. Dakota went with her. Uncle John was in the nursing home. Stretch was at his trailer. Only Young Pal remained. He felt like his existence had stopped and he had nothing more to live for. Jack reached into the glove compartment.

His loneliness was more than one living human being could stand.

Swinging sideways on his truck seat, Jack prepared to step down with both feet together. Jack reached for his cane. Through eyes that were heavy with tears, he saw the porch railing and as each step-and-a-half brought him closer, he knew what had to be done. Balancing his 200 pounds with only slightly more weight on his undamaged side, Jack eyed the porch railing and remembered his grandfather's final bonding with his favorite horse, The Baskir Curly.

Sometimes actions just have to be taken whether right, wrong, approved or disapproved. Seizing his cane at the bent end with one hand on the shaft and the other on the crook, Jack made the same decision about his cane that Joe Steele had made about Curly. Jack's fingers, for one last time, explored the grooves on the cane head that reminded him of Mack's pig eyes and hairy ears. Grandpa had learned to love Curly, but Jack had learned to hate Mack.

Raising the black walnut prize above his head to the full length of his arms, Jack converted sorrow into anger and asked like the Biblical Samson that God would give him strength.

Jack's wood chopping and carnival bell ringing muscles contracted. The North Dakota stillness was broken by the sound of one intense crack.

Young Pal yiked, one of the wood splinters had burned his ribs. Except for the part still in Jack's hand the cane had been changed to kindling. Jack dropped the crook with its Mack-looking head and ground it into the Dakota dirt with his left heel. Steadying his body against the railing, Jack opened the porch door remembering the pact that Uncle John and he had made to keep the ROCKING J going no matter what.

Walking without his cane for the first time in months, Jack was preoccupied with maintaining his gait. He walked by the Illusion horse hide, failing to notice the posted picture and note.

The phone was also ringing incessantly.

"Hello Jack." This time it was not just some woman with a sweet affected voice trying to sell windows. Instead, it was the fantasy phone called he had always dreamed of receiving. The voice was Danni's. "I just wanted to tell you how much Dakota and I enjoyed our visit. He's asleep in the truck or he'd be right by the phone. We're in Moorhead and if I could, I'd turn around and come back home to North Dakota. Dakota and Danni will be coming back to your place next weekend and if you'll have us, we plan on staying there—permanently."

"Damn woman!" Jack still hadn't lost all his post-traumatic freedom of speech. "It sure takes you a long time to learn. I've been waiting for this phone call since the time I saw you follow the snowplow to town. That was nine years ago. You bet! I want you here forever or until I get killed in the next wreck. I was so depressed when I got back to the ROCKING J that I broke my cane. The only person here is young Pal and he's a dog. I can't go on living like this."

"Jack, Dakota is starting to stir in the truck. Hold on. I'm sure he wants to talk to you." Danni left the receiver dangling and she hustled for the Bronco.

"Hi Dad. I just came back alive. Kind of like you did when you went to sleep after Mack tried to kill you. Only I was just resting. Did you see my note on Illusion? It's in the porch." Dakota Frazier sounded like the next Steele generation.

"What note? I didn't see any note." Jack had been so concerned with his own misery and answering the phone that he had completely missed Little Dakota's message that was written with larger than life child printing.

"Just a minute. Hang on. I want to see what you wrote." Jack hobbled, not in step-and-a-half time but double-and-a-half time, to the porch and turned 180 degrees to take an nth look at Illusion.

Back to the phone with tears draining freely down his cheeks and more in his voice, Jack bragged on his son, "That's the best piece of literature I've ever read. Put your mom back on the phone. But before you go, I want you to know that your dad loves you clear up to the sky and way down to the devil and to the inside of the light bulb."

"Surprise! Jack, I just wanted to make sure you saw the picture and the note. Now you understand. It's a sure thing. We'll be back. And I overheard what you said to Dakota, about all the ways you loved him. That was the best way I've ever heard anyone say 'I love you' to a kid. Just in case you're wondering, I loved you even when you were asleep in the care center." Danni was interrupted by Jack.

"Danni, I never told you this, but before I woke up from the coma, there was a Really Tall Guy that promised me that I'd get to see you again. I bet that my sleeping brain recognized you and Stretch. Anyway, I want you to know that I loved you enough to leave Heaven and come back to Earth. I love you more than Heaven. See you next weekend." Jack's voice drifted like a green colt sagging his galloping circle toward the barn.

Clicking the receiver, Jack returned to the porch. This time he spent several minutes looking at the newly refurbished hide of Illusion.

The hide was the same. Like the ROCKING J, it would survive. But something was different. In the center of Illusion's back was a picture featuring the stars of the ranch. Holding the reins of a chunky red- spotted pony was an eight and one-fourth year-old boy. Standing on either side of him, were his mother and father. This was the new ROCKING J family: **Dakota, Danni, Jack and Conclusion.**

~210~

Beneath the picture was a note written on a torn piece of white cardboard that, only hours before, had protected one of little Dakota's Christmas presents from his tricky eyes. Printed with letters squared at the corners and clearly separate from each other were five entirely capitalized words. A child's name was signed in cursive below the note.

I'LL SEE YOU ON FRIDAY.
Dakota

Broadening his smile, Jack reached down to pet Young Pal and check for splinter damage. At last, tranquility covered the kitchen atmosphere. North Dakota chill broke through the ROCKING J ranch house door as Jack carried his kindling to the old wood cookstove. Dousing his cane with diesel fuel, he lit a wooden match by quickly running it over the Wrangler denim that covered his right hamstring. The friction of the match against his jeans caused the end of the matchstick to ignite with sweet smelling sulfur.

Noise from the porch floorboards startled Jack, halting his cremation of Mack's hard walnut head. Stomping boots and a solid door knock were followed by Stretch's automatic entrance. "Thaut I beter cum ovr an jis chek on yu ta see ifn yu waz awrite now dat Danni an Dakota ar gon. Dat dog jis don tak da plac of a gud wuman an a grat ked."

"Glad you stopped over. You got here just in time for the last rites of Mack. Look what happened to my fancy cane." Jack directed Stretch's gaze into the half-opened cookstove firepot. Pig eyes stared from Mack's walnut head that Jack had shoved between the center division of the grates. Mack's ugly head was trapped in steel and his stare menaced like Satan's resurrection on the floor of hell. Squinting upward toward his still living adversaries, the dull evening light sucked the remaining reality from Mack's reincarnation. Bared teeth, chiseled sharp from use, snarled with retracted lips and opened jaws were in ready position to clamp tightly and rip living flesh from tendon and bone.

"Damn! At som bitch loks skary a nuf ta cum bak ta life." Jack's trauma, spinning through his damaged brain begging for subconscious relief, was evident to his loyal buddy, Stretch. "Mack waz da bigst idjit I evr saw. Yu need ta burn dat hors inta hell so yu can be free a da memry a him."

Jack threw the dead match against the cast iron stove grates and dug the bottom of his pocket for another. "I bought these farmer matches just for this occasion. I kept them in the glove compartment of my truck and planned on having a private ceremony. Mack and I were going to have it out. The first time I lost. This time I'll win. I'll be free. Maybe my memory of the wreck will even come back and I'll even win the first fight."

Stretch hoisted the hinged stovetop so the entire burning area was visible. He stood silently for what seemed like the beginning of eternity. Removing his frumpy cowboy hat, Stretch bowed his head. "Giss we gotta hav a praer even fer the devil imself."

The time for cremation had come. Cast iron grates of the 1940's stove, now corroded and burned thin, lay bare except for one cane in the form of black walnut splinters. Jack looked to Stretch for approval. Neither spoke. Another match sparked to life from Jack's thumbnail. A hissing ignition crawled from the match head toward Jack's fingers. Just before the match's fire reached Jack's skin, he coldly dropped the open flame on the diesel fuel. Flaming fuel slowly exploded into a single yellowish-orange flame that rose larger and larger until the kindling caught fire. After the diesel fuel was fully burned, the flame color changed from yellow—to red—to blue—and when the fire was hottest, the flame from the dry hardwood burned white-hot.

When the energy of the wood was nearly gone, the flame changed back to yellow and the toxic smell of burned diesel fuel penetrated the atmosphere. Jack tilted the stovetop cover that was farthest from the smoke pipe to create a back draft that would smudge the kitchen air. Smoking his final breath into the ROCKING J ranch house, Mack's second life dropped into the beginning of forever.

Standing inside a smoky cloud, Jack and Stretch had still not regained their conversation. Coals drew their eyes vacantly into the rectangular space that smoked no more. The demon had died and the possessed had been freed.

Numbed by his trance of joy, Jack removed the only remaining stove lid to the reservoir so he could watch the very end of the vanishing. The last ember darkened and dropped into the ash pot. Mack's black walnut carved head had been completely transformed into heat and smoke and ashes.

Jack turned to Stretch, "Let's get out of this smoky kitchen. Before it gets pitch dark, I want to take another look at this year's crop of weanlings. There's a replica of Illusion in the bunch. Tomorrow morning we'll start training."

Halfway out the kitchen door, Jack glanced back at the silver saddle on the stairway railing. Before leaving the porch of the ROCKING J ranch house, Jack reread the squarely printed letters and signature on the Appaloosa horse hide. Jack's mind, laden with his favorite Dakota memories, made his face smile.

DAKOTA MEMORY SEQUEL
by
Jerry Halvorson

Discover what happens to Jack, Danni and THE ROCKING J. Dakota, Stretch, Uncle John and even the dog, Pal, continue to create Dakota vivid memories.

Horse stories entwine with romance. Ravages of human survival on the ranches of North Dakota extract a high price from the courageous. Mystery characters appear, complicating the family constellation. Economic issues and personal tragedies of unexpected origin cause the plot to thicken.

The final pages of DAKOTA MEMORY provide clues to an unfolding story that is both colorful and picturesque.